HERE'S
ARE SAYING ABOUT
KEITH A. ROBINSON'S
ORIGINS TRILOGY:

Logic's End is a great read, and I highly recommend it. It explores the question of what life would be like on a planet where evolution really did happen. The surprising result helps the reader to see why life on Earth must be the result of special creation. For those interested in science fiction but who are tired of all the evolutionary nonsense, *Logic's End* is a refreshing alternative.

—Jason Lisle, PhD, Astrophysicist
Institute for Creation Research

In this book, Robinson has discovered a 'novel' way to communicate vital information to young adults and readers of all ages. Mainstream indoctrination on the origin of species and the age of the earth are regularly encountered and have long needed combating. Through this unique story, truth is conveyed.

—Dr. John D. Morris President
Institute for Creation Research

Pyramid of the Ancients will challenge you to reconsider the conventional wisdom concerning the history of our world.

—Tim Chaffey, Writer/Speaker
Answers in Genesis, Co-author of
Old-Earth Creationism on Trial

Escaping the Cataclysm is an edge-of-your-seat thrill ride back through time. It brilliantly explains the plausibility of the biblical account of history, especially Noah's Flood. It also explores details of the feasibility of the Ark itself and the Flood's impact on the earth. A great read!

—Julie Cave
Author of *The Dinah Harris Mysteries series*

Picking up where *Pyramid of the Ancients* leaves off, *Escaping the Cataclysm* hits the ground with both feet running. I found my faith renewed again and again as I was reminded of the many arguments that demonstrate why evolution cannot be the explanation for our origins.

—Joe Westbrook
Co-author of *The Truth Chronicles*

LABYRINTH

THE TARTARUS CHRONICLES BOOK 4

LABYRINTH

KEITH A. ROBINSON

OTHER NOVELS BY KEITH A. ROBINSON

THE ORIGINS TRILOGY

Book 1: *Logic's End*
Book 2: *Pyramid of the Ancients*
Book 3: *Escaping the Cataclysm*

THE TARTARUS CHRONICLES

Book 1: *Elysium*
Book 2: *Dehali*
Book 3: *Bab al-Jihad*
Book 4: *Labyrinth*

To all my students, hopefully some of you will get a chance to read in these books what I couldn't say to you in the classroom.

Acknowledgments

My deepest gratitude goes out to the following people:

To Jas Tham, my cover artist, for sharing your talents and making my books look so good!

To Melody Christian, my graphic artist, thank you for squeezing me into your schedule and getting my books done so quickly. You're awesome!

To my wife, Stephanie, you never cease to amaze me. You are everything a man could ask for in a wife.

To my children, I pray that you will always seek the Lord. Let him guide your life.

To my Lord and King, Father, let the work of my hands be pleasing to you and may it draw others into the kingdom.

CONTENTS

1

PURSUIT

The heavy military transport sped through the damaged city of Bab al-Jihad, the vehicle's hover jets gliding smoothly over sections of torn-up streets that were the result of the earthquake that struck the city five days ago. Jade gripped the steering wheel tightly, her eyes rapidly scanning every alley, parking area and garage for signs of pursuit.

Sitting in the front passenger seat, Raptor glanced furtively at the rear camera display while simultaneously trying to direct Jade down the various streets of the city. So far, he and his companions had made it halfway through the city without incident. However, they all knew it would only be a matter of time.

In order to rescue Gunther and Travis from the hands of Imam Ahmed, Raptor, Charon, Xavier, Jade, and Braedon were forced to form an uneasy alliance with the technologically and genetically altered Guardians from Elysium. In exchange for one of the newly developed Implant Disruptors created by the Dehali military, the Guardians created a diversion by attacking the government compound. The diversion allowed Raptor and the others to make their way past the Army of the Ahmed Caliphate and into the group of buildings on the island in the center of

Bab al-Jihad. By using the Implant Disruptor and cutting power to the island, the group managed to get past the AAC's soldiers with their ten-foot tall mechanized suits and rescue their friends. Having escaped the island in a stolen military transport, they now found themselves trying to get as far away from the city as possible before the AAC discovered their location.

As the transport turned a corner, nearly everyone in the vehicle felt a wave of nausea hit them as the feeds to the devices implanted in their brains returned. "Whoa," Xavier said, overcome by momentary dizziness. "Well, it appears our Guardian friends and their wonderful Implant Disruptor have moved out of range. It sure feels good to have it back. What did mankind ever do before the invention of these things?"

"They used phones and commlinks, like many of the 'natural born' still do," Braedon replied. As if to accentuate his point, he pulled out the commlinks that Raptor had acquired for them while their implants were inoperable and flipped it on. "Kianna, our implants are back online."

"Okay," came the reply from the African American woman. "I'll switch over to my translator. It's much easier to use than these clunky comms."

Although she tried to hide it, Braedon could hear the tension in his friend's voice. Hoping to alleviate some of her anxiety, he decided to keep her talking. Opening up a TeleConnect channel with a mental command, he sent his thoughts through the device. *How's Cat? Is she still sleeping?*

Despite being a 'natural-born', Kianna was able to respond to his TC call by using a specialized headset. *Yes, although I think she's beginning to wake up. I'm so glad that sedative you gave her worked. I was anxious enough for the both of us. Having to just sit there in the Spelunker waiting to hear from you was definitely not fun. And, when we were attacked by those soldiers and I had to...to use the Vortex weapon—*Her digitized voice trailed off for a moment before continuing—*I'm just glad she didn't have to witness that.*

Me too. She's been through so much pain and hardship already, she certainly doesn't need to see more.

Yeah. Poor thing. I can't image what it must have been like for her. Just the idea of being captured, bought by a man, and forced to be his wife for ten years freaks me out.

Braedon didn't immediately reply. The reminder of what had happened to his wife since she arrived in Tartarus triggered a myriad of emotions. Brushing them aside, he redirected the conversation. *Hey, Raptor wants to know where you're at right now?*

According to the computer map, we're about five minutes from the cavern's western tunnel. By the way, tell Jade that her pet mindim *has been driving me crazy with all its chirping and squawking! Most of the time, it was curled into a cute, gray, furry ball that was hiding under the seats. But as soon as I started driving it—oh no—*

The lighthearted tone of her voice suddenly became tight and laced with dread, causing Braedon's stomach to lurch. *What is it?* he asked, fearing the answer.

They've found me! What do I do?

As a former soldier in the Elysium Security Force, Braedon had been in situations before where he was alone and under attack. He knew the paralyzing effects fear could have on a person and recognized the telltale signs in Kianna's voice. *Listen to me. You're going to get through this! Keep going as fast as you can toward the tunnel. We're not that far from you, and Charon still has the stolen mechsuit. With his hoverjets, he can be there before we do. Just stay calm.*

When she responded, her voice sounded strained but resolute. *Okay. But tell Charon to hurry!*

Braedon closed down the connection and explained the situation to the others. Immediately, Jade hit the accelerator, throwing caution to the wind while Raptor contacted Charon.

It looks like break time is over. They've sighted Kianna and are following her. She needs help immediately. If nothing else, see if you can slow them down until we catch up.

Got it. And I was just about to stop for coffee.

A second after the sarcastic reply came through the TC channel, Raptor watched as a mech launched into the air several blocks in front of them, hoverjets blazing. *Kianna, this is Raptor,* he said, opening up another channel. *Charon's on his way. How many are chasing you?*

Um, I can't quite tell. I know there's at least one hovercar following me, but I thought I saw a mech unit off to my left somewhere.

Raptor muted the conversation and turned toward Jade. "Have Zei fly around the Spelunker so we can get an aerial view of what we're facing."

"Good idea," the Asian woman responded. A second later, she sent a mental command through her implant to her pet.

What the....? Raptor, Jade's mindim *just jumped out the open window!*

Don't panic. She's having Zei fly around above you so we can use her camera implant to see what we're up against.

Oh, Kianna replied in relief.

"Raptor, the images are coming in," Jade said. "I'm going to forward the camera feed to you. Unless, of course, *you* want to take over and drive this 'tank' through a busy city at high speeds."

"No thanks," he responded through clenched teeth, bracing himself against the dashboard as Jade rounded another corner, her maneuver pushing the boundaries of safety. "You seem to be doing just fine."

"Uh, boss?" Xavier said from where he sat in the back of the transport, his hand running nervously through his wavy black hair. "I thought you might want to know that we've picked up a tail of our own. Jade's erratic and reckless driving has succeeded in attracting some unwanted attention. There are two hovercars behind us filled with some of our AAC 'friends' all dressed up in their finest jihadist-fighter uniforms!"

Jade swore loudly, leaving the con man to wonder if she was responding to his news or to his assessment of her driving skills.

"That's just great," Raptor mumbled sarcastically. "Yeah, they're trying to contact us right now on the comm. Jade, new plan—route the pictures to Xavier and Braedon. You two call Charon and give him the intel. I'm gonna talk to our 'friends' back there and see if I can get them to back off."

Switching over to Arabic, Raptor responded to the urgent call from the militants chasing them. "This is transport three twenty-one. I'm glad you're here. The fugitives have split up! We're pursuing the—"

"Transport three twenty-one," the militant said, cutting him off mid-sentence, "your vehicle has been reported stolen! In the name of Allah, you must pull over right now or we'll open fire!"

Raptor swore and hit the button that cut off the conversation.

"So much for that idea," Jade commented, casting a wry grin in Raptor's direction.

Ignoring her, Raptor grabbed his laser pistol and hit the control that lowered his window. "It looks like we're gonna have to do this the hard way," he shouted as he turned in his seat, leaned out the window, and began firing at the two vehicles behind them. "Braedon, Xavier, talk to me! What's going on with the Spelunker?"

"It's not good," Xavier replied. "Besides the one following her, there are two mech's approaching from the south on an intercept route. And they've set up a roadblock at the west tunnel consisting of two hovercars and a transport."

Raptor didn't immediately reply but instead sent several more shots toward their pursuers. To Xavier's left, Braedon rolled down his window as well and joined Raptor, his own laser pistol spewing forth bolts of energy. "Tell Charon. Have him intercept the two mechs. Then tell Kianna to turn around and head back toward us."

"What?" Xavier asked in confusion. "But I thought—"

"At this point, we need to regroup. Then we're gonna ram the blockade!"

2

COLLISIONS

"What?" Kianna said into the microphone of her implant translator.

He wants you to turn around, Xavier said.

"But I thought—"

He changed his mind. There's a blockade up ahead waiting for you. You need to regroup with us or you'll never make it.

Kianna swerved quickly to avoid hitting a car in front of her and instead sideswiped two other vehicles parked nearby. Pedestrians scattered everywhere as she sped down the narrow street. "Okay," she replied, once the congestion was behind her. "What street do I take?"

Turn left then make another left at the second intersection. You should see us coming toward you in a minute.

Kianna followed his instructions and turned the Spelunker at the next intersection. Just as she rounded the corner, she nearly slammed on the brakes in surprise. Leaping over the rooftops to the southwest were two mechs heading directly for the tunnel exit only a dozen blocks away. Stunned, it took several precious seconds for her brain to realize that she didn't seem to be their primary target. Frustrated at herself for panicking, she hit the accelerator once again.

"Xavier, I just spotted two mechs heading toward the tunnel!" she yelled into the translator.

Don't worry about it. Charon's got it covered.

Kianna frowned in confusion. Suddenly to her amazement, a third mech leapt up from the street level and crashed directly into one of the others in midair.

The initial impact rattled Charon, causing him to nearly lose consciousness. However, the gamble had been worth it. His mech's momentum and trajectory altered the course of his target by forty-five degrees. The two men, encapsulated inside their metal suits, crashed into the side of a building, nearly tearing a hole straight through the outer wall. Having been expecting the collision, Charon recovered quicker than his opponent. Due to the close quarters, he knew many of his ranged weapons would be useless. Pulling back one of his suit's metallic arms, he began to pummel the other suit like a jackhammer.

With the mech's pilot on the defensive, Charon took a moment to check his arsenal. When he'd first commandeered the suit, the Implant Disruptor had been in effect, forcing Charon to learn to pilot the machine without the mental connection. Once the Guardians moved out of range and the feeds returned, he hadn't had time to properly integrate his personal implant with the suit. As such, when he went to activate his mech's laser cutter, he accidentally turned on the wrong weapon.

A rocket suddenly shot out from his suit's right shoulder and slammed into his opponent's armored chest at point blank range. Realizing what he had done, Charon quickly leapt backward and hit his hoverjets just as the rocket exploded. The resulting shockwave caused him to lose control of his jump, sending him hurling toward the street below.

He hit the ground hard and once again found himself fighting against unconsciousness. After finally recovering from the jolt, he slowly forced himself to stand. However, before he could fully regain his balance, warning sirens blared, indicating that he was being targeted. Glancing to his left, he realized too late that the first pilot's partner had found him.

"Here comes the Spelunker!" Xavier called. "C'mon, Jade, you've gotta time this just right."

"I know what I'm doing!" she yelled back as her hands gripped the wheel even tighter.

"Yeah, I know that much! But you're also trying to glance at the images coming from Zei's camera while driving at the same time! It's not like you've had a lot of practice doing this sort of thing."

"So shut up so I don't have to do both while also carrying on a conversation! Here we go! Everyone, brace for impact!" Jade called out, as their transport neared an intersection.

The image of the Spelunker racing past their front windshield on a perpendicular street caused them all to flinch involuntarily. A second later, the AAC hovercar that was pursuing her began to cross in front of them. Although Jade's timing had been good, she only managed to hit the rear of the car as it passed instead of full side-on collision. The result, however, was enough to send the car careening into a wall, taking it out of the chase.

"Nicely done," Raptor said with relief as Jade maneuvered the heavy transport back onto the main road.

"Now what do we do about the ones that are still chasing *us*?" Braedon asked as he prepared to open fire once more on the two AAC cars behind them.

"For now, we keep shooting at them," Raptor replied. "We may not be doing much damage, but we're at least causing them to keep their distance."

"If only I could get the rest of the traffic on these streets to keep their distance!" Jade said through gritted teeth as she swerved once more to avoid another car.

"What about Kianna?" Braedon asked. "Where's she at now?"

Xavier's eyes lost their focus for a moment as he communicated with her through the TeleConnect channel. "She has turned back around and is following behind our pursuers! She's chasing the chasers!"

"Good. Tell her to stay close. I've got an idea."

Charon expected to see lasers, missiles, or rockets come streaming toward him at any second when, to his amazement, the other pilot spun his mech around to face a side street. Then just as the man was preparing to fire at some new target, he abandoned the attack and activated his suits hoverjets. Although his quick actions kept him from being slammed full force into the heavy military transport that came tearing down the street at him, he was still thrown off balance by the attack. Instead of leaping straight into the air, he flew at an angle and crashed head first into a nearby tree.

Meanwhile, the transport suddenly slammed on its brakes, coming to a halt. As Charon watched, the hovercars pursuing the transport slowed down and were preparing to stop when the Spelunker came from behind and rammed into the rear of the second vehicle, sending it crashing into the first.

Shaking off his brush with death, Charon leapt into action. Using his targeting computer, he locked onto the mech in the tree and sent a volley of laser fire toward his opponent, doing enough damage to take him out of the fight. Then, just as the group of AAC soldiers from the two cars were beginning to recover, Charon activated his suit's compressor. The wall of sound waves crashed into the soldiers causing them to collapse into unconsciousness.

Hey, Charon. Glad to see you're still with us, Raptor said through the implant once they all had a moment to catch their breath.

Glad to still BE with you. If you guys had showed up a second or two later, I would've been roasted! I see you also managed to find the ladies as well. Now what do you say we get out of this blasted city once and for all?

Sounds good to me.

The AAC guards at the roadblock tensed as the transport came into view. "Watch it, men. Here they come. Remember to keep an eye out for that rogue mech."

The commander glanced around to make sure everything was in place. He knew that his own heavy transport and two hovercars blocking the entrance to the western tunnel should be more than adequate to prevent the criminals from simply plowing through the blockade. And between the two tripod-mounted heavy lasers and the firepower from the other six men in his command, they would undoubtedly win a firefight.

"They're not slowing down, sir!"

"Hold your positions and prepare to fire!" he shouted.

The commander narrowed his eyes at the approaching vehicles. Clearly, these fugitives were desperate, but he had also been warned that they were clever. Something wasn't right about this. He was just about to give the order to fire when he recognized his mistake.

With the vehicles traveling toward the blockade head on, he had failed to notice that the rogue mech was actually clinging to the back of the transport. At this distance, the vehicle itself, which had no weapons of its own, wasn't a threat. But the mech was a completely different matter.

Two missiles screamed over the roof of the oncoming transport. The commander barely had time to warn his men to take cover when the first of the missiles slammed into the ground in front of the tripod lasers, causing them to topple onto their sides. An instant later, the second missile slammed into the transport, carving a giant hole straight through the middle of the vehicle.

Stunned by the sudden attack, the commander and his men watched helplessly as the mech pounded what was left of the transport with laser fire. As the approaching vehicle neared the blockade, the mech leapt off the back just before it plowed its way through the two hovercars and the remains of the destroyed transport. The resulting impact of the collision crushed the entire front end of the attacking vehicle.

However, it succeeded in opening a path for the hovering Spelunker that followed behind.

Stunned by what had just occurred, the commander cried out in fury as the Spelunker pulled around the wreckage. Immediately, the driver of the ramming transport jumped out of it and climbed into the second one.

"Stop them before—"

He never had a chance to complete his thought. The mech pilot, having regained his focus from his jump, suddenly activated his sound compressor. The commander watched his men fall where they stood, their weapons clattering onto the pavement.

Then, he watched as the compressor turned in his direction. The last thing he saw before unconsciousness stole over him was the Spelunker driving swiftly down the tunnel, followed close behind by a small flying mammal.

3

GHOST STORIES

There was an audible sigh of relief and an immediate release of tension as the Spelunker moved deeper into the tunnel away from the blockade.

"Thank the Celestials!" Travis whispered. "We made it!"

"Nice trick, Raptor," Braedon said with respect. "I've gotta hand it to you. I really thought they'd see the five of us switching from the transport into the Spelunker and know something was up."

"We're also glad you weren't injured in the crash," Kianna added.

Raptor fought against the grin that was trying to work its way into his expression. "It's easy enough to survive a hit like that when you know it's coming. Those things have built-in restraints. I can tell you, those force generators really work. I barely moved an inch when I hit."

"That's a whole lot more effective than those airbags they used to use on Earth at the beginning of the twenty-first century," Gunther commented.

Once they were far enough down the tunnel, Jade slowed down just long enough for Zei to catch up. Once the chattering *mindim* was safely inside, her owner hit the accelerator to resume their escape.

Next to Braedon in the middle section of the vehicle, Catrina let out a groan and opened her eyes sleepily, the sudden stopping and starting of the Spelunker rousing her. Still not fully awake, she stared around at the others in a daze. Noticing Braedon's arm around her, Gunther frowned in surprise.

"So who might this be? It seems that our little 'band' has gotten a new member while Travis and I were away."

Braedon smiled. "Gentlemen, I'd like to introduce you to my wife from Earth, Catrina Lewis."

At this revelation, both men stared in surprise then frowned in confusion almost simultaneously. "Your wife?" Travis asked. "But I didn't know you were even married. Where...where was she while we were in Dehali?"

Braedon filled them in on how he and the others discovered that she had been sold as a wife to a Muslim jihadist and how they had rescued her. By the time he had finished relating the tale, Catrina had become fully awake. Smiling sheepishly, she reached over the back of her seat and shook the hands of the two men sitting beside Xavier.

"It's a pleasure to meet both of you," she said, her green eyes and shoulder length, tousled red hair added to her relaxed inno-cence, causing them to immediately warm up to her. "Braedon speaks very highly of you and has told me so much about you and your families. Is it true that you can get us back to Earth?"

The question burst the momentary calm and tranquil atmo-sphere that had settled onto the group, bringing them all back to reality with a harsh snap. "We believe so," Gunther answered. "However, we have learned that the space/time wormholes that open from Earth are focused in only a dozen or so locations. These are the *only* areas where portals can form. So we have to be in one of these locations for the Vortex to work."

of the Well. Retrieve another copy of the map to the Labyrinth, and upload it to the commanders. Send them through the maze to the Well as fast as possible to apprehend my son and his friends! They must not escape!"

4

ENTERING THE LABYRINTH

The group eventually began to relax as the computer driver piloted the Spelunker farther and farther away from the city. From time to time they stopped, allowing everyone to stretch, including Charon who continued to insist on piloting the mech suit. Finally, after nearly a full day of travel, they reached the edge of the Labyrinth.

"Really? This is it? Are you sure?"

Raptor glanced back at Xavier. "What did you expect? Flashing lights and warning signs?"

"Well, not necessarily. But it…it just looks like every other average tunnel."

"Yes, but unlike the other tunnels, which are mostly man-made, and thus smoothed out for travel, these are natural. And once we pass through this opening, there are numerous other tunnels that split off every hundred feet or so."

Raptor, I should take point. If we do encounter some of Xavier's beasties, at least I'll be able to use the suit's weapons to scare them off, Charon said through his implant.

Good idea. But don't forget to switch over to using the commlink. Once we enter, we'll lose our implants.

Figures. I had just finished connecting mine to the suit a couple of hours ago.

Keep an eye on your motion sensor and search every side tunnel. We don't want anything getting the drop on us, Raptor instructed. *We should be able to avoid most predators as long as we stick to the map and watch our motion detectors.*

Got it. Let's get this over with.

"Okay, everyone. Here we go," Jade announced as she shut down the computer driver before following Charon across the threshold.

The main entrance was easily fifty feet wide, leaving plenty of clearance space for the Spelunker to drive, its gravity generators casting their bluish light onto the purplish walls. Ahead of them, Charon's mech walked confidently, its brilliant white search lights blazing a path through the darkness.

No one spoke as they moved deeper into the maze. As Raptor had stated, other tunnels appeared regularly, some as wide as their current tunnel, others not much larger than two feet in diameter. Charon paused at each one, his arm laser leading the way as his search lights probed for signs of danger.

Raptor sat in the passenger seat and used the holographic map to chart their course. Behind him, Xavier and Braedon took turns watching the motion detector. They had only been in the Labyrinth for thirty minutes when Braedon saw a blip appear on the display, indicating that something was far down the tunnel behind them. He was about to share the information with Raptor when, to his surprise, the blip disappeared. Frowning, he tapped the machine.

Noticing his confusion, Xavier glanced over at him. "What's wrong?"

"Probably nothing. Hand me one of the other detectors. This one seems to have some kind of glitch."

"What makes you say that?" the con man said suspiciously.

"For a second there, it showed movement down the tunnel behind us, then it was gone."

"Maybe we should check it out. We don't want anything following us."

Braedon exchanged devices with Xavier, turned the new one on, and returned to studying the screen. "If I see it again, we'll look into it."

Xavier shrugged and let the topic drop. As time dragged on and the blip didn't reappear, he and Braedon began to relax, considering the anomaly to be simply a glitch. Eventually, the group began to strike up conversations while Travis and Gunther did their best to begin calibrating the Vortex weapon, despite the lack of proper working room inside the cramped vehicle.

Several hours passed by uneventfully. "Charon, we're going to take a break for the night," Raptor announced through the comm. "According to the notes on the map, there's a cavern nearby that should be safe enough. In order to get there, we need go down to the next level. Up ahead about three hundred feet or so, there's a hole large enough for the Spelunker."

"Glad to hear it. I've really gotta use the bathroom!"

Raptor grinned. "Yeah, you're not the only one. The good news is that there's also a small freshwater stream running through that cavern. We can refill our water containers there."

A few minutes later, Charon reached the indicated area. An enormous chasm forty feet wide and seventy feet long opened up in the floor on the left side of the main pathway. Ahead, the tunnel continued and split again, one passage heading upward at a forty-five-degree angle, the other heading straight.

After checking for any signs of danger, Charon lifted the arm of his mech in a salute. "All clear. See you at the bottom." Without another word, he activated the hoverjets on his suit and disappeared down the chasm.

"How are we going to follow?" Catrina asked, her anxiety spiking. As a result, she winced in pain and put a hand on her abdomen.

Noticing her reaction, Braedon's brows furrowed in concern before responding. "Don't worry. The Spelunker lives up to its name. Just watch."

Jade drove them to the edge of the hole then activated the vehicle's 'legs'. Immediately, a dozen metal tubes extended out from hidden compartments located around the front, back, and sides of the Spelunker. The designers had created the tubes in such a way that they could collapse, allowing them to fit inside each other when retracted. But as they extended, they snapped into place and locked together. Made of an extremely durable yet thin metal discovered in Tartarus, the legs each contained individualized hover generators and were able to extend up to twelve feet each. When combined with the nearly ten foot width of the Spelunker itself, the total reach was just over thirty feet.

Once the legs were extended, the computer diverted power from the main hover generators to the legs, causing the vehicle to rock slightly. After it stabilized, Jade slowly piloted the Spelunker over the hole. Catrina let out a short scream and gripped Braedon's arm painfully as the vehicle dipped precariously to the left. However, the legs mounted on that side finally came within reach of the far side of the fissure and brought the Spelunker level once more. Because of the hole's somewhat rectangular shape, the legs in the front were forced to swivel to the sides to find purchase. With all twelve gravity generators pushing against the walls of the chasm at forty-five-degree angles, Jade kept a close eye on the displays from the cameras mounted underneath the Spelunker and began their descent.

They moved steadily downward for eighty-five feet. Twice, Jade was forced to adjust some of the legs to avoid outcroppings that jutted out from the walls of the pit. After ten minutes of tortuous rocking, shaking, and controlled falling, the Spelunker reached the bottom of the fissure.

"Brace yourself, everyone," Jade called out. "This last part gets a little tricky."

The moment Jade hit the button on the console, the computer changed the angle of the dozen extended legs until they pointed almost straight down. The sudden change caused the Spelunker to lurch drastically. This time, Catrina wasn't the only one to let out a gasp. Kianna, Gunther, and Travis all found themselves caught off guard by the maneuver. However, within seconds, the main gravity generator kicked in, bringing their descent to a gentle halt on a cushion of air. A few moments later, the legs had retracted, and the main display on the pilot console indicated that they were ready to drive once more.

"So *that's* what it feels like," Gunther commented, a slight edge to his voice. "I'd seen holos and videos of trucks and cars doing this but never experienced it myself."

"Me neither," Travis stated, his face pale. "Let's hope we don't have to do that again anytime soon."

"Don't count on it," Raptor said. "We'll likely have to use the legs quite a bit more before we reach the Well."

"Ha. If you think going down was bad, wait until we have to go *up!*" Jade added.

"Is it just me, or is she enjoying our discomfort a little too much?" Xavier quipped.

"How did these tunnels form anyway," Kianna asked.

Raptor shrugged. "Who knows? Some think it was from lava that flowed through here thousands of years ago."

"I read somewhere that it was probably from a large body of water that was suddenly released into this area," Travis said as Jade started them moving down the tunnel once more. "Like a dam that burst, the water carved out these tunnels in a matter of hours as it rushed downhill toward the Well. In case you didn't notice, we've been traveling downhill most of the way from Bab al-Jihad. In fact, I wouldn't be surprised if the cavern that houses the city was originally where the water came from. Over the years, the water found alternative pathways, leaving these tunnels dry."

Now that they had begun moving forward again, Braedon grimaced as Catrina loosened her grip on his arm. Seeing his pain-filled expression, she looked down and recoiled in sudden dismay and remorse at the small cuts and indentations left on his wrist by her nails. "Oh, Braedon, I'm so...I'm so sorry! I didn't mean to—"

"It's okay," he reassured her. "They're just scratches."

Her head drooped, and her gaze fell. He could tell by her body language that she had erected an emotional wall again. Sighing, he stared out the window and began to pray.

It wasn't long before the tunnel widened into a large cavern filled with beautiful white crystalline shapes about three feet long that stuck out from the floors and ceilings, except for the fifteen-foot-wide roadway that had been cleared through the right side of the tunnel. Flowing down the center of the cavern was a gentle stream about fourteen feet across. The beauty of the crystals was enhanced further by the fact that they each pulsated with an inner light, which reflected off the water and onto the walls.

Everyone in the group was mesmerized by the lights as they drove into the chamber. "Look at how they pulsate in ripples or waves!" Kianna commented. "It's almost as if they are....breathing!"

"Who would've thought that the Labyrinth would contain such beauty," Gunther added.

"Yes, but don't let it fool you. Stay alert," Raptor said.

As soon as Jade brought the Spelunker to a halt, the group filed out, weapons in hand. Only after they were satisfied that there was no immediate danger and that the water was safe, they set about refreshing themselves. Jade's pet *mindim* immediately flew down to the stream and began splashing around playfully, taking away a little of the heaviness that weighed on the group.

Xavier watched the creature with a grin as he crouched at the water's edge and filled his canteen. However, the grin vanished the moment he noticed Raptor approaching. One quick look at the other man's face told him that this wasn't going to be a pleasant conversation. In fact, he knew immediately what was coming. He had been dreading this conversation.

Hoping to soften the blow, Xavier spoke quickly as he stood. "Look, Raptor, I…I know what you're gonna say. I—"

Raptor grabbed the man by the front of his shirt and pushed him painfully into one of the large crystals. "I warned you," Raptor said. The coldness in his voice sent shivers down Xavier's spine. "I told you to stay away from those Pandora's Box parlors, but you just couldn't do it. You're a filthy addict. Now because you had to blab our location during one of your sessions, things are way harder than they should have been. Gunther and Travis never would've been captured, we never would have had to go to Bab al-Jihad to rescue them, and we wouldn't be traipsing through this cursed Labyrinth! Because of you, we may not succeed, and tens, perhaps hundreds of thousands of people might die!"

Guilt and shame overwhelmed Xavier, causing him to wither under Raptor's accusations. "I know! I'm…I'm so sorry! I promise it'll never happen again! I give you my word!"

Raptor sneered. "Your word is trash. You promised me the same thing in Dehali."

"But this time—"

"Shut up!" Raptor snapped. "If I didn't need all the help I could get, I'd throw you down the nearest hole and leave you to die. You'd better hope we succeed. And if we do make it out of this alive, I don't ever want to see your face again. You got it?"

Xavier nodded rapidly. Raptor instantly let go of him and stormed away, leaving the man shaken and ridden with self-loathing. Ignoring the looks from the others, Raptor strode away from them and found a place to sit by himself near the stream.

Lost in his anger, it took him several moments to realize that he wasn't quite as alone as he thought. He could just make out the sound of two hushed voices over the sounds of the gurgling water. Glancing over, he noticed that Braedon and Catrina were sitting on some rocks at the water's edge just on the other side of several large crystals. Although he didn't particularly want to listen to their private conversation, he also didn't feel like moving anywhere else. So instead, he tried to simply ignore them and study the map of the Labyrinth. However, before long, he found himself being drawn to their conversation.

"Why are you so nice to me?" Catrina asked, her voice low. "Why didn't you snap at me for hurting you?"

Stunned by the question, it took Braedon several seconds to reply. "Cat, you know I'd never treat you the way he did."

"I'm starting to understand that," she said, looking up at him with a small grin. "But even the old Braedon wouldn't have put up with me the way I am now."

"That's because I was a young, selfish idiot. And trust me, the new me still has his flaws. The changes you see in me are because of Jesus."

"What?" she asked, confused. "What's that supposed to mean?"

"Being a Christian is about so much more than just following a bunch of rules, Cat. It's about having a relationship with Jesus."

She raised her eyebrows questioningly. "How do you have a relationship with someone you can't see or hear?"

Braedon smiled. "I may not see him physically or hear him audibly, but I get to know him by reading his Word. The Bible is a complex book. But in many ways, especially with the New Testament, it is like a collection of love letters. The most famous verse in the Bible sums it up, 'For God so loved the world, that he gave his one and only son, that whoever believes in him will not perish but have eternal life.' He loves us, even when we've turned our backs on him or rejected him. He still loves us and is waiting for us with open arms."

Catrina looked down. "Maybe for you. You don't...you don't know the things I've had to do to survive. He may welcome some, but I doubt he'd want me."

His heart filled with anguish over the pain his wife had experienced. "That's not true. God is the God of the broken-hearted! The Bible says that *nothing* can ever separate us from the love of Christ. The amazing thing about our Creator is that *he* gives us worth. We have no worth on our own. Yet he loves each of us so much that he was willing to pay the penalty for every wrong thing we've ever done. All we have to do is ask him for forgiveness for our sins and accept the free gift he offers."

"That sounds a lot more comforting than the God I heard about growing up," she replied wistfully. "He was all about 'do's and don'ts', rules, laws, and condemnation."

Braedon put his arm around his wife and drew her close. "Honey, that's because we were taught wrong. Read the Bible for yourself. You'll see."

"Well, if he can make this much of a positive change in you, then I guess I could at least hear what he has to say," she said, raising her eyes to look into his. For a moment, she hesitated, then, before she could change her mind, Braedon leaned down and kissed her gently.

On the other side of the crystals, Raptor stared at the ground, completely ignoring the holographic map of the Labyrinth that still shimmered over the device in his hand. Instead, his thoughts and emotions dwelled on Braedon's words.

Suddenly, a loud chirping echoed throughout the chamber. Glancing toward the source of the noise, Raptor frowned as he saw Zei perched on one of the crystals looking down at something on the ground.

A moment later, Jade, Kianna, Travis, and Gunther stopped what they were doing and strode over to where the creature was still chirping loudly. "What is it, girl?" Jade asked, as she and the others arrived and examined the area.

Travis suddenly let out a shout. "We've gotta get out of here!"

Now fully alarmed, Raptor jumped to his feet and ran over to where the man was pointing and backing away from something. "What's wrong? What is it?"

As if struck dumb, Travis merely pointed at several objects on the ground near the stream. Raptor stepped cautiously toward it, his laser pistol at the ready. When he saw what had startled the scientist, he frowned in confusion. "What are those? They just look like a couple dozen large rocks."

Gunther came up behind him, took one look, and froze, his face turning pale. "Those are eggs! This is a *rizak* nest!"

5

RIZAKS

"What?" Kianna asked as her eyes darted around the cavern searching for movement. "Are you sure?"

"Yes!" Gunther replied. "I remember watching this documentary about them. Do you see the way the eggs are arranged in a circle and leaning in slightly toward the center? Only *rizaks* do that."

"But according to the map, their nesting grounds are several levels up and much closer to the Well," Raptor said. "There's no record of there being any sightings...."

His voice trailed off as a thought surfaced. As if reading his mind, Gunther nodded. "Just like the *svith* that attacked us on our way to Dehali! The instability in Tartarus is driving them from their normal nesting grounds. If the tear in time and space is focused at the portal entry point next to the Well, then the *rizaks* would naturally migrate away from it."

"Uh, guys, this is all fascinating and such, but the motion detectors just blipped!" Xavier stated, his eyes glued to the device's display. "I've got four objects about five feet long approaching from the tunnel straight ahead of us. At the current rate they're moving, they should be here in just under a minute!"

Spurred to action by Xavier's words, Jade grabbed Zei and put the small mammal on her shoulder as she and the rest of the group bolted toward the Spelunker and Charon jumped back into his stolen mech suit. Raptor held the passenger side door open until everyone else was inside. He was just about to climb in himself when he saw the first of the beasts enter the cavern.

Their wide, flat heads looked out of place with their lithe, muscular bodies. Wicked looking claws several inches long protruded from each of their four toes, which were set into their paws with two in front, two in back. Although they had thick black fur covering most of their hides, their legs protruded from the sides of their bodies like those of lizards. Trailing behind them was a thick, stubby tail that resembled a heavy club.

Catching sight of prey near their nest, the first of the creatures opened its toothy maw and let out a gurgling roar of challenge.

"Go! Go!" Raptor called out before leaping into the Spelunker.

"Where?" Jade asked as she turned the vehicle around to head back the way they came.

"For now, just take us back up to the other level."

"Can't we fight them off?" Kianna asked. "Between Charon's mechsuit and our lasers, we should be more than a match for them."

"Yes, probably," Raptor replied. "But these nasty buggers spit out this really sticky gunk that is *extremely* hard to remove. If they hit the Spelunker or the mech with that stuff, it could put us out of commission. We can't take that chance. Better to run and hope that once we've left their nest area they'll give up the chase."

Grabbing the comm, Raptor hit the button. "Charon, cover our escape. Keep your distance."

"You don't have to tell me. I've seen the holos. I know what these overgrown critters are capable of."

Looking out the back window, the others watched as Charon raised his suit's compressor and fired it toward the pack of *rizaks*. The sound waves hit the four creatures, causing them to reel back in pain. However, after several moments of writhing, they seemed to adjust to the attack.

Charon swore and began backing up quickly toward where the Spelunker had just exited the cavern. "Blast it! I was hoping the compressor would work on them the way it works on humans. It slowed them down, but I think it just ticked them off instead. I'm gonna try the lasers."

Turning his suit around, Charon activated his hoverjets and flew toward the exit. Once he landed, he spun around and prepared to unleash a volley of laser fire toward the animals when his comm crackled.

"Charon, this is Braedon. Don't aim for the creatures themselves. Instead, try hitting the crystals on the ceiling!"

Adjusting his aim, Charon targeted the glowing crystals. As the laser fire hit them, they exploded, sending shards flying in all directions and dropping several of the larger ones down onto the pathway. Caught off guard, the beasts howled in pain as slivers of glass fell on top of them.

Without waiting to see the full outcome of his attack, Charon turned his mech around and sprinted down the tunnel after the retreating Spelunker. "Nice call, Soldier Boy," Charon said into the comm. "Although I didn't stick around long enough to ask them how they were feeling, I can say with certainty that it'll at least slow them down and make them think twice about pursuing us."

"We're still not taking chances," Raptor replied. "Let's head back up the fissure."

"Got it. I'm right behind…." Charon finished his sentence with a curse. "It looks like two of them are still on the hunt.

They're obviously dealing with multiple cuts on their claws, but they're still coming."

"We're heading up now."

Charon glanced up ahead to see the Spelunker's legs extended once more. The twelve gravity generators were all turned down. Then, with a sudden burst of energy, they launched the vehicle twenty feet into the air like a rocket. The height was just enough to reach the bottom of the fissure. With precision that only a computer could achieve, the legs rapidly angled out to catch the walls. Once stabilized, the Spelunker rapidly ascended up the chasm.

"C'mon, hurry up," Charon said as he watched the vehicle rise slowly. Focusing his attention on the approaching creatures, he continued firing his laser at them. To his utter frustration, the *rizaks* didn't just run toward him on the pathway. Instead, they used their claws to climb the walls and cling to the ceiling. As they did so, they ducked into crevasses, hid behind stalactites, and took cover between rocks.

Just as they were closing to within thirty feet of his location, Charon heard Raptor's voice come through the comm. "We're all clear. Get out of there!"

Needing no further prompting, Charon activated the hoverjets on his mech suit, launching him up the fissure. However, due to the difficulty of navigating upward through the rocky terrain, he was forced to go slower than he would have liked.

He was halfway up when his right hoverjet began to sputter.

Caught off guard, Charon careened into the right wall. He began to slide downward but managed to catch his robotic foot on a small ledge. Trapped there momentarily, he reached out with his arms to steady himself. It was then that he noticed the readout on his display. He swore profusely, then glanced down the crevasse to see that the *rizaks* had followed him and were less than twenty feet below.

"Raptor, I've got a serious problem here! I think they got one of my jets! I'm—get away from me you—AAAHHHHH!"

In his frenzied effort to ward them off, Raptor sprayed laser fire down the crevasse, managing to dislodge one of them. He watched in satisfaction as it plummeted to the ground far below. However, during the attack, he lost sight of the second one. Spinning around frantically, he caught sight of movement to his left. Turning his spotlight in that direction, he saw that the thing had gotten slightly above him and was coiled and ready to pounce.

In a panic, Charon raised his left arm and launched one of his last missiles at the creature just as it leapt. The missile narrowly missed its target and instead exploded against the far wall. The *rizak* hit him full force, knocking him off the small ledge. He desperately tried to use his left hoverjet to slow his descent. However, the determined creature had latched onto his suit, the claws digging deep into the metal.

Together, the two combatants fell down the chasm as an avalanche of rocks set free by Charon's wayward missile hurled after them to bury them alive.

6

BURIED

"Caleb!" Raptor cried out, the seriousness of the situation causing him to dispense with his best friend's code name. Even
before the dust had settled, he leapt out of the Spelunker and
ran toward the edge of chasm. Desperate, he shined his flashlight downward, searching for signs of movement. "Caleb? Can
you hear me? C'mon, give me a sign!" Raptor said into the commlink. When no response came, he felt a wave of sickness twist
his insides.

Seconds later, Jade, Xavier, and Braedon ran up to stand
beside him, their own beams of light joining Raptor's. However, even their high powered flashlights were no match for the
darkness of the deep fissure.

"We have to go down!" Raptor said urgently.

"How? The explosion broke loose that huge section of wall!"
Xavier stated, using the beam from his flashlight to highlight the
enormous chunk of rock that had split off and become wedged
against some outcroppings and now covered a large portion of
the chasm. "We'd never get the Spelunker down there!"

"And even if we did, that piece could break off at any
moment!" Jade added. "If that falls while we're down there, we'd

be crushed! And what if one of the *rizaks* survived? They'd tear you apart!"

"What about Zei? Can she go down and search for us?" Raptor asked, his mind working rapidly.

Jade shook her head. "No. It's too dark. Her camera implant wouldn't pick up anything without light." Still clinging to her master's shoulder, the *mindim* looked intently at them, as if she understood that they were talking about her.

"I'm not leaving him!" Raptor growled. "I'll go down with a Pit Climber by myself then!" Turning, he raced off toward the vehicle.

"I'll go with him," Braedon stated. He began to turn but was stopped as Jade grabbed his arm.

"No, I'll go. Caleb has saved my life several times. I'm not just going to sit by while he needs help."

"Jade, be practical. If Charon is still alive and injured, Raptor's going to need someone else to help lift him. We may also have to move some heavy rocks just to get to him. I mean no offense, but I'm stronger than you physically. And Xavier's shoulder is still healing from when he was shot during the escape."

"Yeah," Xavier said as he gripped his wounded shoulder. "I'd be the first one down there, but....you know."

Ignoring the comment, Braedon continued staring at Jade. "You have to admit, I'm the best candidate."

The Chinese woman narrowed her almond eyes at him before finally conceding defeat. "Fine. Just...be careful."

Surprised by her sudden shift of attitude, Braedon gave her a brief smile, glanced at Xavier, then headed after Raptor. Reaching the vehicle, he watched as Raptor was rapidly sifting through the gear to find items he'd need and stuffing them into a backpack.

"What's going on? What happened to Charon?" Gunther asked, worry etched on his face.

"He and one of the *rizaks* fell back down the chasm," Braedon replied. "Raptor and I are going down after him." As he finished this last statement, he looked over at his wife, who had suddenly gone pale.

"Braedon…," she began before her words were choked off by a wave of fear.

Taking her hand in his, Braedon crouched down next to where his wife sat inside the Spelunker. For a moment, the two just stared at each other in silence. "I'll be all right. Pray for us." With that, he leaned in and kissed her gently.

"Here," Raptor said, abruptly ending the tender moment. "If you're coming with me, you can carry our gear. I've got the Pit Climber."

Kianna, Gunther, and Travis all voiced their concern and wished them luck as Raptor and Braedon turned and headed determinedly toward the pit without speaking a word. As they walked, Raptor tried once more to contact Charon but again received no response.

Jade and Xavier still stood at the edge of the crevasse, their lights probing the darkness. As the two men approached, Jade turned toward them. "Based on what we can see, I think your best option would be to descend over there. It looks to be the most stable and has the most clearance."

Although he didn't acknowledge her comment, Raptor nevertheless strode over to where she indicated. Reaching the spot, he grabbed the Pit Climber in both hands and hit the button to unfold it. Instantly, the three-foot-long, thick pole doubled its length. In addition, four curved sections along the base unfolded until they were at ninety degree angles from the central pole. Within seconds, the four sections snapped together to form a sturdy, circular disk about four feet in diameter.

Once the Pit Climber was ready, Raptor set it down on the ground like an upturned, flat umbrella. Stepping onto the disk, he motioned for Braedon to do the same. Both men held onto the central pole, which was now six feet long and several inches thick. "Keep the commlink channel open, and watch the motion detectors carefully," Raptor instructed Jade and Xavier before pressing another button on the pole.

The moment he did so, eight thin metal rods an inch in diameter extended out from the circular base of the Pit Climber. As with the legs on the Spelunker, each of the rods ended in a gravity generator. Within seconds, Raptor and Braedon were lifted up on cushions of air created by the eight devices. Using the guidance levers built into the side of the pole, Raptor navigated the Pit Climber and its two passengers over the precipice and began their descent.

A holographic display of what lay below them was projected from the pole, allowing the two men to watch with agonizing slowness every detail of their descent as the computer built into the unit maneuvered their way down the chasm. Several times, the Pit Climber was forced to adjust their trajectory to avoid the numerous outcroppings and rocks that jutted out from the walls.

Suddenly, they heard the sound of rock grating against rock coming from above. A second later, a shower of dust and dirt poured down on them.

"Hey, what was that?" Raptor said through the commlink once the dust had settled.

"You'd better hurry!" Jade said, her voice uncharacteristically filled with tension. "That entire wall section just shifted about half a foot! We don't know how long it'll stay in place."

The two men exchanged quick, knowing glances. "Understood."

Trying not to think about the tons of rock that could potentially drop down on them from above, Raptor and Braedon instead tried to focus on the task at hand.

Not content with just relying on the lights and images projected by the machine, Braedon leaned over the edge and shined his high-powered flashlight downward. Finally, after what seemed like hours of stressful uncertainty, they reached the bottom.

Raptor halted their descent as they neared the pile of rubble that had been caused by Charon's failed attack. Below them, covered by several large rocks and mounds of dirt, they could see the right arm and the tail of the first *rizak* as well as the crushed head of the second one that had attacked Charon.

"There!" Braedon called out suddenly as the beam of light from his flashlight reflected off the unmistakable metallic object sticking out from the debris. "I think it's one of the legs of his suit!"

"It looks like most of the rocks and dirt spilled out into the tunnel below instead of getting piled up in the pit itself," Raptor commented as he studied the area.

"We're extremely lucky that large portion of the wall remained intact and got wedged on those outcroppings. Otherwise, we never would've made it down here."

"We'll have more room in the right passage. I'll get us over there." Deactivating the computer on the Pit Climber, Raptor piloted the device over the rubble and down to the floor of the tunnel.

The moment the disk came to rest, the two men each turned on a glow lantern, filling the area with a yellowish-gold hue. Raptor attached one of the lanterns to the top of the Pit Climber, then the two of them jumped off it and headed toward the rubble pile. "We've reached the bottom and can see part of the leg of the mech suit," Raptor said into his commlink. "We're attempting to dig him out now."

"Okay. Hurry up!" Xavier replied.

The two men reached the area where the metal leg protruded slightly from the rubble. Braedon set his lantern down, then they set to work removing several large rocks from the area. "Hang on, buddy," Raptor said between clenched teeth as he hefted another boulder out of the way.

They had cleared away enough of the rubble to free up the legs of the suit only to discover that an oval-shaped giant boulder nearly six feet in diameter rested on top of the suit's torso. "Raptor, the legs seem intact, but do you...do you think the armor held? That seems like a lot of weight...."

"No, it held. These things are designed to take a lot of pressure. If he even had one hoverjet still functioning enough to slow his fall, the suit should have been strong enough to protect him from the debris falling on top of him."

Suddenly, they heard a weak voice coming from inside the suit. "You could...always ask the...the guy in the suit."

"Caleb, you idiot!" Raptor cried out in relief. "I told you to stay away from the *rizak*!"

"Yeah, well, ...I never was... any good at...following directions."

"Are you hurt?"

"I.... don't know. I can't move."

"Hang on. We'll have you out of there in a minute."

"We? Don't...don't tell me you brought....Xavier with you."

Raptor glanced at Braedon as the two continued to remove the rocks. "No, his arm is injured, remember?"

"He's probably...using that as an....excuse. I bet....Wait a second, you...you brought...Soldier Boy!"

"Hi, Charon," Braedon said. "I'm glad to see you're still alive."

The large man coughed briefly before finding his voice again. "Yeah, I bet. Just shut up and get me outta here!"

They worked frantically for several long minutes while continuing to give updates to the team waiting anxiously above.

Finally, Raptor stopped and stared at the enormous boulder, his mind searching for an answer. "It's too big. How are we gonna get that thing to move?"

Braedon shook his head. "I don't know. We need to get some kind of leverage on it. We need a pole or—"

"Wait!" Raptor called out as sudden inspiration struck him. "The Pit Climber!" With renewed urgency, he slid hurriedly down the debris pile and grabbed the device. A few moments later, he arrived back where Charon remained trapped. "Help me brace the top of the center pole against the wall here."

"What...what are you guys...doing?"

"Hang on. With any luck, this will get that boulder moving. If we can get it off you, we should be able to get you out."

With the bottom disk of the Pit Climber pointed directly at the rock and the top of the pole wedged into the wall, Raptor activated the legs of the unit and manually directed them toward the boulder. "Get ready. Here we go!"

The second he hit the activation switch, he and Braedon had to fight to keep the device horizontal as the gravity generators kicked in. Fortunately, they didn't have to hold it for very long. The combined force of the generators pushed against the boulder, sending it crashing down the debris pile and into the opposite wall of the tunnel.

Another rumble came from above, causing Raptor and Braedon to dive toward the side passage as more rocks and stones dropped down on them. "Are you guys okay?" Jade asked through the comm. "We heard a crash and then that wall section shifted again!"

Dusting himself off, Raptor grabbed the comm. "We're fine. We used the Pit Climber's gravity generators to move the boulder off Charon. It worked, but it shook things up a bit down here. We'll be on our way up again in just a minute. Hang on."

Shutting down the comm, he and Braedon climbed the pile once more until they were standing beside the mech, which was now nearly free. "Charon, your arm's still stuck, but we're going to try to open the suit. Hopefully, you can get your arm out without a problem. Otherwise, we'll have to cut it off."

"WHAT?"

"I'm just kidding. But we do have to hurry. That wall you knocked loose is still threatening to drop on us. Nice work, by the way."

"Yeah, whatever. I'm sure you'll...never let me...live this one down."

Hitting the manual release, Braedon and Raptor were forced to pull hard on the damaged metal of the suit in order to get it open far enough for them to reach their friend. After several minutes of struggling, the three of them managed to extricate Charon from the suit.

Once free, the three men paused for a moment in relief, their chests heaving from exertion. "You look terrible," Raptor stated, noticing with some concern the various cuts and bruises on his companion's face and arms. One eye seemed somewhat swollen, and his left leg had a deep cut across his thigh from where the suit had sliced him. In addition, his left arm, which had still been trapped in the suit under the debris, was badly scraped and battered.

"I still look better than you," Charon replied with a wry grin.

"C'mon, let's get back up there," Braedon said. Standing up, he retrieved the Pit Climber and set it up on the floor of the side passageway.

"Um...how are we gonna do this?" Charon asked. "That thing can only hold two of us."

Raptor glanced at Braedon, but the other responded before he could say anything.

"You take Charon up then come back down to get me."

Surprised, Raptor nodded, his respect for the man increasing. He knew it was no simple thing to agree to stay down in the darkness all alone, especially with the potential collapse of the wall above and *rizaks* lurking around.

It took them another minute to help Charon and Raptor get situated on the Pit Climber.

"Here, take this other lantern. Keep your motion detector on and your laser ready. I'll be back for you as soon as possible," Raptor instructed.

Just as Braedon was preparing to step back from them, Charon reached out with his good arm and clapped him on the shoulder. "Thank you, Braedon. I owe you one."

Braedon smiled up at the large man. "You're welcome."

Stepping back, he watched as Raptor and Charon rode the Pit Climber up the rubble pile. Then, with one last glance in Braedon's direction, the two men disappeared into the shaft. Alone in the darkness save for the two lanterns and his flashlight, Braedon sat down next to the large boulder that had previously pinned Charon. With the wall at his back, the boulder on his right, and his motion tracker in hand, he settled in to wait…and pray.

"We've reached the top," Raptor reported through the comm after several long minutes of oppressive silence. "I'm on my way back down."

Braedon stood, collected the two lanterns, and stood near the bottom of the chasm, doing his best to remain calm. Above, he could see the light from the Pit Climber growing larger and larger.

Then, to his utter horror, he felt the floor beneath him begin to shake. "Oh no…please. Please not now!"

The intensity of the shaking increased rapidly, leaving no doubt in Braedon's mind what was happening. The earthquakes that Gunther and Travis had predicted were starting!

7

DETOUR

"Raptor, drop!" Braedon yelled. "That wall section is—"

Before he could say any more, the ground beneath him heaved, sending him sprawling onto the rubble. He fought against the rolling rocks in a desperate attempt to get further into the western tunnel. Seconds after he got out of the way, the Pit Climber came into view.

In a last ditch effort to beat the collapsing wall section, Raptor had deactivated the device's gravity generators, sending him into a brief free fall. Then, just as he neared the top of the rubble, he reactivated them. However, his timing was off just enough that one of the generators crashed hard against the rocks. The disc upon which Raptor rode tilted unexpectedly due to the damaged leg.

Several large rocks flew past him as he struggled to regain control of the Pit Climber. Above, he could hear the thunderous roar of the wall section as it combined with the rumble of the earthquake itself. Fighting desperately against his rising panic, Raptor wrestled with the stubborn machine until he finally managed to get it headed toward Braedon's lights. He had almost cleared the opening when another huge boulder smashed against one of the Pit Climber's legs with enough force to bend it downward. The crooked leg tipped the disc once more, this time causing Raptor to lose his balance and fall off. He landed hard on his left knee then rolled until the sharp stones on the floor dug painfully into his back, halting his momentum.

Dazed and delirious from the sudden pain, Raptor was barely conscious enough to realize that Braedon had arrived at his side and was dragging him to safety. Suddenly, a deafening boom filled the tunnels and dust flew up his nose and clogged his ears. He felt Braedon's hold on him slip as he fell to the ground just ahead of him.

For several moments, the two men could only lay on the debris as the world around them shifted. Gasping for air, they covered their mouths and noses with their shirts as dirt and small pebbles pelted them, as if seeking vengeance for disturbing their slumber.

They lost track of time as they lay in the pitch black darkness that enveloped them. Slowly, the rumble began to recede. Even once the earth had returned to its dormant state, the two men remained motionless, overcome with an irrational fear that any movement would reawaken it. At last, their comms crackled to life, startling them out of their lethargy.

"Braedon? Please…please respond and tell me you're okay. You can't leave me like this!"

Roused by Catrina's urgent pleas, Braedon hit the comm and replied, his mouth dry and scratchy. "Yes…yes, honey, I…I'm okay."

He heard her audible sigh come through his earpiece. "Thank God! When the earthquake started and the wall collapsed, I—we thought you may have been crushed! The others want to know if you saw Raptor. He was on his way down when…when the wall fell!"

"He's"—Braedon coughed and choked on the dust that still lingered in the air—"I think he's....okay. He made it down just in time but got knocked off the Climber. I dragged him a little farther into the tunnel and out of the way." Reaching over, he felt Raptor's pulse. "He's pretty bruised and beat up, but I don't think he broke anything. It's...it's really hard to see right now because of all the dust. I dropped my flashlight, and I think the lanterns are buried, although there's some faint light coming from somewhere."

"Hang on," Jade said, cutting in on the commlink channel. "I'm going to use another Climber to work my way down."

"Okay, but I'm not getting my hopes up. From what little I can see, the debris from the earthquake is filling the entire area. I think we're gonna have to find another way to get back up." Switching off the comm, he leaned toward Raptor, who still appeared to be unconscious. "Hang in there. I'll be right back. I'm going to see if I can get us some light."

His body ached as he stood and brushed the dust off his clothes as best he could. Feeling around in the near darkness, Braedon slowly made his way toward the faint light source. "I think the light is coming from one of the lanterns," he said into the comm. "Now that the dust is starting to settle, I can see a couple of other lights coming from Raptor's climber."

"That's great news!" Gunther replied. "Kianna's studying the map right now to see if we can find another route to get to you."

Braedon reached the light source and began working on extracting the lantern from its rocky grave. After a minute of digging, he managed to free the durable object. Although the outer casing was cracked, the bulb was still shining brightly. Now that he wasn't fumbling in the dark, he climbed over the rubble until he reached the Pit Climber. After a quick examination, he did his best to fold the device back down to its smaller storage and carry size. However, due to the damaged gravity generator on one leg and the bend in the other leg, he couldn't collapse it completely.

At the edge of his consciousness, Braedon could feel his own panic and fear threaten to overtake him. The thought of being trapped or lost in the stifling tunnels of the Labyrinth made his heart pound and his stomach twist. Fighting against a sudden sense of claustrophobia, he turned on the comm once more, hoping the conversation would take his mind off his predicament. "I found Raptor's Climber," he reported. "It looks a little rough, but I think it'll still function."

"Good, because it appears you're going to need it," came Jade's reply. "I've made my way down the crevasse, and…I'm sorry, but there's no way we can get to you through here. We're gonna have to find another passage that connects."

"Yeah, I figured as much," Braedon said. Hoisting the Climber onto his shoulder, he started carefully crossing over to where Raptor was now sitting up and leaning against the wall. "Gunther, Kianna, …tell me you've got… some good news," Braedon said, panting from the strain of carrying his burden over the uneven ground.

"Well, it's not great, but it could be worse," Kianna replied. "There's a large vertical shaft similar in size to this one that leads up to this level, but it's several miles to the east, which is back the way we came."

"What about…is there anything…west?" Raptor said into the comm as Braedon reached his side and set down the Pit Climber.

"It's good to hear your voice," Xavier chimed in. "For a minute there, I thought we were going to have to find someone new to boss us around and growl at us."

Kianna's voice cut back into the channel, cutting off any sarcastic reply that might have been forthcoming. "There appear to be several smaller shafts not too far ahead to the northwest.

But in order to get there, you have to go down another level first. And....according to the map, there's a nest of Viper Lizards in that vicinity."

"How close?"

"The nest itself is several hundred feet south of the tunnel that leads to the shafts. But Travis says that they likely hunt in that area. Then again, if they've moved their nests like the *rizaks*, they might not even be in the area at all. They're only a foot tall, but he said that they swarm their prey and overwhelm with numbers. If you run into even one of them, they'll alert the pack."

Raptor swore before responding. "Then it looks like....we'll have to backtrack." With supreme effort, he climbed slowly to his feet, wincing in pain as the blood rushed to the cuts and bruises on his legs. "We're going to try to ride on the Pit Climber. With any luck, we'll be there shortly."

"Sounds like a plan. Jade's coming up out of the chasm now," Xavier said. "Once she's on board, we'll be on our way."

"Tell Charon he owes me big time for this one."

Xavier grunted. "I would, but Travis gave him something to help with his injuries, and it also knocked him out. He actually slept through the whole earthquake! So you'll have to tell him yourself when he wakes up."

"Whatever. Braedon's setting up the Climber right now. We'll check in a minimum of every ten minutes."

"Take care of yourselves," Kianna said. "And let us know each time you reach an intersection so we can make sure you're still on track."

"Got it."

"Braedon?" Catrina's voice suddenly came through the commlink.

Pausing the setup of the Pit Climber, Braedon clicked on the comm on his wrist. "I'm here, Cat."

"Please be careful. I...I just wanted you to know that...I love you."

Braedon felt a warmness spread through him. Ever since her rescue, he wasn't completely sure if the spark could be rekindled. This was the first time she had uttered the words. As quickly as it came, the warmth evaporated and was replaced by heartbreak. *What if I never see her again? What if there's another earthquake and....* He expelled the thoughts from his mind before they could do any more harm. Swallowing hard, he spoke into the comm, "I love you too. See you soon."

With the conversation finished, Raptor turned toward his companion. "Well, let's get this over with."

Together, the two men got the device setup and working. Although it took them several minutes to adjust their weight so they could balance on the damaged device, they finally figured it out and got it moving down the tunnel.

The bent leg and loss of one of the gravity generators caused the Pit Climber to constantly drift erratically, forcing them to travel slower than they would have liked. As they went, Braedon steered while Raptor kept watch on their motion detector.

They had traveled just over twenty minutes when the edge of their lantern light illuminated a sight that caused their hearts to drop into their stomachs. "No, no, no!" Raptor said in disbelief.

Bringing the Pit Climber to a stop, Braedon closed his eyes momentarily before activating his comm. "We've run into a problem. We're not going to be able to make it."

"What's wrong?" Jade replied, her voice tinged with concern.

"The tunnel has collapsed."

8

DARKNESS AND LIGHT

There was silence for several seconds after Braedon's announcement. Finally, Kianna's voice came through the commlink. "We were afraid of that. Gunther mentioned the possibility of tunnel collapses due to the earthquake, but we didn't say anything because…well, we didn't want to bring it up. You had enough to deal with already."

"Right. So what do we do now? Is there another way around?"

"Yes, but they're all very far off, and each go through several known lairs of dangerous animals. I'm sorry, Braedon, but based on the map, your best bet is the one that leads near the Viper Lizard nest."

Raptor and Braedon exchanged concerned glances. "It doesn't look like we have a choice," Raptor said. "We understand. We're heading back."

"Since it looks like we're going to be down here longer, can you find us a source of fresh water?" Braedon added. "We're both starting to feel a little dehydrated."

"Got it. There are a couple of places that look promising," Kianna replied. "Since we can move faster than you, we'll go on ahead and make sure the earthquake didn't leave us any more surprises. If possible, we'll even try to come down and meet you halfway with some food."

Braedon offered their thanks and closed down the channel. "Back to square one," he commented, then piloted their damaged Pit Climber back the way they came.

In the dark confines of the Labyrinth, time seemed to lose all meaning. The only thing that broke up the monotony of travel was that they had to keep in regular contact with the others to make sure they were still on track due to the frequency of forks in the tunnels. After several turns and dips in the terrain, Kianna was able to lead them to a small stream where they were able to refresh themselves and wash away some of the grime from the tunnel collapse. Invigorated by the cold water, they continued their journey through the stifling confines of the Labyrinth.

Lost in the bowels of Tartarus, the two men lapsed into silence, their thoughts turning to recent events and the near future. Despite his best efforts to the contrary, Raptor soon found himself returning to Steven's prophecy and its connection to his recurring nightmare. *These tunnels look uncomfortably similar to the ones in my dream. Could I have somehow manufactured the nightmare based on images I saw somewhere of the Labyrinth? The walls here are darker than others I've seen in the rest of Tartarus, just like in my nightmare. And is it any coincidence that, according to Steven's prophecy, I've only got two more days left to live, which is exactly how long it'll now take us to get to the Well.*

With his mind afflicted with confusion and doubt, he found himself longing for something solid to hold on to. *I feel like a blind man stumbling through a huge, empty cavern, desperate to reach out and touch—something—anything to use as a fixed point of reference. But instead, all I get is more darkness with each step.* Glancing over at his companion, Raptor suddenly realized that he envied the man. Overcome by his sense of despair, he found himself searching for anything to take his mind off his thoughts.

"So tell me, how did you and Catrina meet?"

Braedon turned and studied his companion, surprised by the sudden question. He could tell that something was bothering the man but decided not to probe. "We were high school sweethearts, even though I was a couple years older than her. I was a junior when a buddy of mine introduced me to this really cute freshman. She was so shy. I remember being stunned by her green eyes and wavy red hair. It wasn't long before we were dating. However, things were rocky from the start. We fought a lot, mostly because I was a jerk."

"Weren't we all at that age?"

Braedon grinned. "I suppose we are. But despite it all, she still put up with me, even after I graduated and joined the military. My father was a major in the army before he died, which is probably why he wasn't the most compassionate or gentle of men. Yet for some reason, I still wanted to follow in his footsteps."

"How old were you?"

"Fourteen. I was in a depression for my first two years of high school. In a way, dating Catrina helped me to deal with my father's death. I was so selfish back then. I unloaded a lot of my baggage on her. She was tough, though. She gave as good as she got when we fought. We were married shortly after she graduated."

"How long were you married before you...came to Tartarus?" Raptor asked, seeing a side of Braedon he'd never imagined.

"After our first couple years of marriage, we knew we were in trouble," Braedon said, his voice filled with emotion. "The trip we took to India was our last try at fixing our marriage. We knew if something didn't change, we'd end up divorced. As usual, we got into a heated argument, and I stormed off into a secluded area to be alone. When the portal appeared, it sucked me in. What I didn't know was that she had followed me. She saw what had happened and ran toward me, but was too late to keep me from getting pulled in. Instead, it got her as well."

"Only you didn't know."

"Right. Without Steven's friendship, I don't think I would've recovered. I remember just wanting to die."

"I'm glad I never had to experience that," Raptor said. "I was born here in Tartarus. I don't know what's worse—never having seen Earth but hearing all these wonderful stories about it, or having seen it but been pulled into Tartarus."

"I think I would've preferred to have never seen it. Being trapped underground after having known the sun and sky is hard to deal with."

The two halted their conversation long enough for Kianna to direct them through the next intersection. Once they had moved on, Braedon turned to the other and asked a question of his own. "Your turn. There's been something bothering me since we left Elysium—why are you helping us? And don't give me that line about Tartarus collapsing and wanting to help save people. You didn't even know about that stuff when we were in Elysium. Even more, you looked truly spooked when Gunther used the Vortex and it almost killed you."

Raptor felt his anxiety rise at the memory of the incident. "What do you expect? Facing death tends to have that effect on people."

"It was more than that."

For an instant, Raptor felt a wave of irritation pass over him at the line of questioning. He was about to tell the other to mind his own business when a new thought expelled the other one. *After all you've been through together, why not tell him about the prophecy and two signs? Hasn't he proven himself to be trustworthy?* Making up his mind, he told Braedon about his conversation with Steven back in Elysium. When he had finished, he could see that the other was deep in thought.

"Wow," Braedon said at last. "Now I see why you were so willing to even fight Charon on this. Don't take this wrong, but based on your lack of religious belief, I'm somewhat amazed that you took Steven's prophecy seriously."

"Yeah, I've asked myself the same question," Raptor said. "But the truth is, I don't have any other explanation for it. Honestly, I'm still not convinced. I guess I was initially spooked, and I might have left you guys in Dehali if we hadn't found out that Tartarus really was collapsing. At this point, I'm just going on self-preservation."

There was a lull in the conversation as both men became lost in their own thoughts. After a moment, Raptor broke the silence and resumed the conversation. "Speaking of self-preservation, I've got to ask—how can you be so sure of your faith that you were willing to give your life for it, even if it meant leaving your wife alone?"

Braedon took several moments in order to decide how best to respond. However, when he did, he spoke with a calm assurance. "Steven once said, 'If you don't stand for something, you'll fall for anything.' I realized a long time ago that the only things in life worth living for are the same things worth dying for."

In the yellowish light from the lantern, Raptor could see in Braedon's eyes a sense of peace that made his soul ache. Unaware of his companion's perusal, Braedon continued. "As I told you before when we were in Elysium, what many people fail to realize is that religion is more than just a set of laws and rules. Every religion is a system of truth claims. Once you become convinced of the truth, the next logical step is to conform your life *to* those truths."

"Much like the jihadist who puts on a suicide vest and blows himself up to kill infidels because he believes it is one of the only ways to earn the favor of Allah," Raptor said softly.

"Exactly. But there are many who claim to believe, but when difficulties arise, their beliefs take back seat to their desire for things of this world," Braedon continued.

"Let me guess, you're speaking of Xavier."

Braedon turned to look at Raptor in order to gauge his sincerity. He was mildly surprised that he detected no trace of sarcasm or defensiveness in the other man's demeanor, only genuine curiosity and openness. "That's right. Xavier may claim to believe in God, but he hasn't reached the point where the truths of Christianity impact the decisions he makes and the course of his life. His is more of a pragmatic faith. He takes the parts that make him feel good and ignores the parts he doesn't like."

He paused in his explanation as they neared another fork in the road. Once they confirmed with Kianna and the others which direction to take, Raptor resumed the discussion.

"I've always thought that most religious people had the kind of faith that Xavier has. That's why I've always despised them. They're hypocrites. They say something is wrong then contradict their own statements by their actions."

"Sadly, that's true for too many," Braedon replied. "But if those people truly grasped the reality of what the Bible teaches, it would change their lives. Jesus was unlike anyone who has ever lived! He proved it by living a life that was above reproach. His enemies tried numerous times to trap him, but he always responded in a way that left them with nothing. They examined his actions with a fine-toothed comb but couldn't catch him doing anything wrong.

"In fact, even those opposed to Jesus confirm his claims," he continued, encouraged by Raptor's attentiveness. "The Roman government had all the resources and power they needed to find his body and persecute his followers, yet they couldn't stop Christianity from spreading. The Jewish leaders recognized

I'm guessing you'd love nothing more than to see me drop on my knees and make some kind of confession of faith."

Braedon smiled. "I don't know about the whole 'dropping on your knees' thing, but...yeah, I'd say you are starting to understand me."

"Well, I've seen and experienced some things since I've met you that are causing me to rethink what I've always been told, but I'm just not ready to stake my life on any set of religious beliefs."

"Look, I understand and respect that. But keep in mind, none of us are promised even another day of life. The way things are going," Braedon continued with a disheartened expression as he glanced at their surroundings, "we may not even survive this day, or even the next few minutes. And, considering what Steven said in his prophecy, I wouldn't wait too long."

To punctuate his words, Braedon brought the Pit Climber to a halt. Before them, the tunnel sloped sharply downward at more than a forty-five-degree angle. "This is it." Flipping on his commlink, he contacted the others. "Kianna, we're here. We've reached the edge of the Viper Lizard hunting grounds."

9

HUNTING GROUNDS

"Got it, Braedon," came Kianna's reply through the commlink. "We're almost to the tunnel that connects to yours. It took us longer than expected because we had to go around two cave-ins."

Charon's voice suddenly burst loudly through the speaker, cutting off anything else Kianna may have wanted to say. "Raptor, you idiot! I can't believe you got yourself into this new mess."

"Yeah, you're welcome," Raptor said, his tone humorously defensive. Despite the seriousness of the situation, he couldn't help being relieved at the sound of his best friend's voice. "You gave us quite a scare. And just for the record, Braedon and I are in this mess because you have terrible aim! You should never have hit the wall with that missile or, for that matter, let that *rizak* get close enough to spit his goo on your hoverjets!"

"Whatever," he said dismissively. "I...uh...I guess I owe you one."

"You owe *both* of us. I never could have gotten you out of there without Braedon."

"Yeah, well, I guess I owe one to you too, Soldier Boy."

"What was that?" Braedon replied jokingly. "I didn't quite hear that last part. Could you repeat it again?"

"If you didn't hear it the first time, that's your fault. I ain't repeating it," the big man stated gruffly.

Raptor and Braedon shared a brief laugh, thankful for the respite from the oppressiveness of the Labyrinth. After a moment, Jade spoke, the soberness of her words putting an end to the jovial atmosphere.

"You two had better get moving. In case you had forgotten, there could be another earthquake at any time, and we have the entire AAC army hunting us."

"Thanks for the reminder, Jade," Raptor said sourly. "Pardon me if I'm not so eager to go sloughing around through some narrow caves that could be infested with Viper Lizards. Then again, I am starving. The sooner we get back to you, the sooner we get dinner!"

Kianna returned to the conversation. "You'll want to take the tunnel to the left. It should be one that slopes at just over a forty-five-degree angle, right?"

"It looks that way," Braedon replied. "And of course, it would have to be the narrowest, most treacherous path. That seems to be my luck lately."

"Sorry about that," she apologized. "It slopes downward for quite awhile, taking you to the lowest 'level' of the Labyrinth. However, you won't be down there long. Once the tunnel levels out, you don't have far to go before you reach the tunnel that leads to the shafts that'll bring you back up here."

"If we don't get swarmed by a pack of hungry Vipers," Raptor added casually.

"We've been thinking about that," Jade said. "The tunnels down there aren't as wide as the ones higher up. They're only about fifteen feet wide and some narrow to as little as five feet. If you run into a hunting pack, you might be able to fire your laser pistols at the walls or ceiling to break free some stalactites to cause a small cave-in."

"If the earthquake didn't do that already for us. As far as we know, any of these tunnels could lead to dead ends...literally."

Xavier chimed in. "Hey, the docs say you should probably narrow your beams and keep your lantern dimmed. Use the motion detector to alert you. They said that your lights would make it easier for them to find you. On the *bright* side—get it?—if they do find you, crank up your lights. It might blind them momentarily."

"Thanks, professor," Raptor said. "We'll keep that in mind. C'mon, Braedon. Let's get this over with."

Braedon acknowledged his statement by urging the damaged Pit Climber toward the sloping tunnel.

"And one last thing," Kianna said. "Don't talk unless absolutely necessary, and use your comm's earpieces instead of the speaker. I guess these Vipers have really good hearing. So when you reach an intersection, click the comm three times, then click it again with the number of tunnel openings."

"Got it," Raptor whispered, heeding her advice. He and Braedon paused for a moment to insert their earpieces before continuing on. As Kianna indicated, the tunnel dipped sharply, causing them to have to extend the legs in the front of the Pit Climber while keeping the back ones short in order to remain level. In addition, the tunnel narrowed to the point where the two men could almost stretch out their arms and touch the walls with their fingertips.

They traveled in silence deeper and deeper, their senses alert and on edge. The closeness of the tunnel gave them a sense of claustrophobia, enhancing their anxiety. They held their breath at each intersection, praying that the motion detector would remain dormant.

After nearly an hour of travel and its accompanying suspense, they were greatly relieved when they arrived at the bottom. Grabbing his comm, Raptor clicked it three times to signal the others, then clicked it four more times to indicate that four tunnels split off from their current one.

"Good. You've arrived at the nexus," Kianna said through their earpieces. "The floor should be more level here, right? One click, yes. Two clicks, no."

Raptor clicked once.

"Okay. You need to take the *second* tunnel on the right. It winds around a little then leads to another nexus with four tunnels."

Thankfully, the tunnel Kianna indicated was slightly larger than the one which brought them down. However, this new cave was damp and humid, with small craters of bubbling and steaming water scattered around the floor. As they moved deeper in, the vapor began to coalesce into a fog that limited their vision.

The heat and humidity within the tunnel made breathing difficult. Soon, both men were drenched with sweat and moisture. Raptor quickly removed his *svith-scale* jacket and tied it around his waist. Braedon followed suit and removed his jacket as well. It didn't take long for their mouths to become dry from dehydration.

Suddenly, Raptor leaned over in alarm and showed the motion detector's display screen to Braedon. A quick glance was all he needed to see that the fog was interfering with the device, making them effectively blind.

They slowed their movement to a crawl, straining against the mist for signs of movement. Mostly blind by the combination of fog and darkness, Braedon stayed near the wall of the cavern and watched the slight reflection of his lantern on the dark-purplish stone. A sudden scraping sound of metal against rock jolted the two men and sent their hearts thumping rapidly in their chests. Reacting instantly, Braedon stopped the Pit Climber and backed away from the large hidden boulder that had scraped the underside of one of the metal legs.

For a dozen heartbeats, the men remained frozen in place in fear, their ears sifting through the sounds of the water dripping and gurgling for any signs that they had been discovered. Finally, Raptor rapidly motioned for Braedon to continue their trek.

They had barely moved another dozen feet when they heard the earth begin to rumble once again. Because of the gravity generators on the Pit Climber, they didn't feel the earthquake, but heard it and watched with horror as rocks and stalactites began falling from the ceiling. An enormous cracking sound coming from far off behind them could be heard above the rumble. Accompanying the sound was a rush of hot air and the distinct smell of sulfur and brimstone.

"Go!" Raptor shouted to be heard above the earthquake.

Braedon pressed on, desperately trying to maneuver the stubborn machine through the hail of small rocks that were pelting the weary travelers.

"C'mon, don't collapse," Raptor said as he watched the ceiling above them for any signs of weakness. As the rumble of the earthquake began to fade, Raptor turned his attention away from the ceiling and began focusing solely on the motion detector.

It was then that he heard the sounds.

"What…what is that?" he whispered to Braedon.

"I don't know. It sounds like—"

"—like hundreds of little reptilian feet slapping against the ground, right? They've found us! We're being hunted! We've gotta go faster! Punch it!"

"I can't see where I'm going! If I speed up, I'm bound to run into something!" Braedon stated in frustration.

"It's either that or we're going to be dinner for a pack of slimy reptiles!"

"Maybe we can try Jade's suggestion of causing a cave-in with our blasters, especially if the earthquake weakened it," Braedon said.

"I don't think it'll work, but we can try. The tunnel's probably too wide. The sound is getting louder. They're definitely gaining on us!" Taking out his laser pistol, Raptor aimed at the ceiling and fired. The laser blast struck the rock ten feet behind their position. The blast only succeeded in knocking a stalactite out of position and sending it crashing to the floor. Swearing, he continued to fire behind them as Braedon steered them as fast as he dared down the tunnel.

"Braedon, Raptor, are you okay?" Kianna's asked through the comm channel.

"For now," Braedon replied. "The earthquake didn't damage our tunnel as far as we can tell. But we have another problem."

"Oh no," she said, her voice filled with dread. "The Vipers found you!"

"You got it!" he replied as he yanked on the controls and barely avoided colliding with another cone-shaped stalagmite that stuck up from the floor of the cave. "Hey, we just arrived at another junction. Which way? Left, middle, or right?"

"Left!"

He turned the Pit Climber and headed into the new tunnel. "Maybe we can lose them here. If not, at least this section doesn't have that blasted fog." With his vision cleared, Braedon risked more light ahead of them. The tunnel narrowed to twelve feet across, forcing him to increase the gravity generators on several occasions in order to float high enough to clear the tops of several large boulders that were in their path.

"They're still getting louder!" Raptor stated. "I think—"

Suddenly, to his horror, the edges of the motion detector's display screen lit up with movement from behind them.

And not just motion, a *lot* of motion.

More and more of the tiny blips spilled onto the display and pressed ever closer to the center. "I don't think we lost them at that last intersection!" Raptor said into the comm. He continued pouring blast after blast into the ceiling, hoping to find a weak point.

"Braedon, Raptor? What's going on?"

Ignoring Kianna's distraught question, Braedon called out to his companion. "Turn up the lantern! Jade said it might blind them enough to slow them down!"

Abandoning his attempts at creating a small cave-in, Raptor grabbed the lantern and turned up the brightness. It was then that he could finally see what pursued them.

The floor of the tunnel was filled with the foot-long Viper Lizards, all frantically charging toward the two humans. The creatures were aptly named. They had the bodies of lizards, but had extremely long necks that resembled those of snakes. And like their reptilian brethren, their venom was deadly.

"Braedon? Talk to us! Are you okay?"

Raptor felt a surge of panic unlike anything he'd ever experienced before. It was one thing to get shot in a gunfight, but quite another thing to be eaten alive by tiny reptiles in a dark tunnel in the middle of nowhere.

"Go faster!" he called out to Braedon. He quickly shut off his comm then used his pistol to send a flurry of laser bolts toward the pursuing pack.

"I'm pushing it at much as I can! That bent leg and damaged generator are making it difficult to—"

Two of the metal legs on the right side of the Pit Climber suddenly struck hard against the top of a broad rocky outcropping that jutted out from the wall. The speed at which they were traveling caused the device to spin wildly out of control and fling its two riders off the central disc.

Braedon and Raptor hit the ground hard, momentarily dazing them. Raptor was the first to shake off the impact. He looked around to see the now unmanned Pit Climber hovering quietly several feet further down the tunnel. Off to the right, the lantern lay on its side near the wall.

Finally, he turned to look behind him toward the source of the cacophony of high pitch squeals. There, only thirty feet away and swarming rapidly in his direction was the pack of Viper Lizards.

Panic overwhelmed him at the sight of the approaching creatures. Scrambling to his feet, he stumbled toward the lantern. "Braedon! Braedon, get up! They're almost here! We've got to—"

Fumbling with his laser pistol and engulfed by panic and adrenaline, Raptor let out a scream of rage and fired at the pack of approaching lizards as fast as his finger could manage. But his efforts failed to slow the wild creatures even slightly.

Brought to consciousness by his companion's yell, Braedon stared at his surroundings in confusion. Then, just as his brain registered the danger, he only had enough time to raise his hands over his head as the Viper Lizards reached him.

10

LAKE OF FIRE

Braedon and Raptor curled into balls just as the first of the tiny reptilian creatures climbed onto them. The two men braced themselves for the inevitable searing pain of numerous fangs and poisonous venom.

But to their utter amazement and shock, the bites never came. Instead, the swarm ignored the two humans and ran right over them. Within seconds, the last of the pack had moved beyond the reach of the lantern light.

Only then did Raptor and Braedon dare to move. Stunned by the sudden turn of events, the men sat motionless for nearly a full minute.

"What the….? What…what happened? I thought…" Raptor muttered at last.

"They just ignored us, but…but why?"

Their bodies shaking from their brush with death, the two men slowly stood. Reaching a shaking hand toward his commlink, Raptor turned it on. "You guys aren't gonna believe this but…but the pack of Vipers just climbed over us as if we didn't even exist."

"What? Oh, thank God you're okay!" Kianna replied. "We thought for sure you—"

"Wait! Did you say they just ran right over you?" Gunther asked, his voice tight with worry.

"Yes!" Braedon said. "Why?"

The channel was silent for a moment before Gunther returned. "You need to get out of there right now!"

Moved to action by the fear in Gunther's voice, the men grabbed the lantern and headed for the Pit Climber, their eyes scanning the tunnel around them for some sign of danger. As they looked behind them, they noticed a faint light reflecting off the walls far down the tunnel.

"What's that?" Raptor asked urgently.

"I don't know, but I don't want to stick around to find out."

Once the two men were back on top of the Pit Climber and headed down the tunnel, Raptor returned to the commlink. "We're moving again, but there's a faint glow coming from the cave behind us, and it seems to be growing brighter. Any thoughts?"

"It is as I suspected," Gunther replied. "The Vipers weren't hunting you—they were fleeing from something else!"

Braedon and Raptor exchanged quick, worried glances before Raptor responded. "Fleeing? But what are they running from?"

"During the earthquake, did you feel a sudden blast of hot air?"

"Yes. It was already stifling before, but now we can barely breathe. Why?"

"The earthquake split open a fissure beneath the Labyrinth. The tunnels down there are rapidly filling with molten lava!"

At Gunther's pronouncement, the two men glanced once more behind them. Although the curves of the tunnel had previously hindered line of sight to their pursuer, the current section was nearly straight, allowing them to see for the first time the deadly red and black liquid as is oozed around the far corner.

"Kianna, how far until we reach the shafts?" Braedon asked as he tried to keep his attention focused on the path ahead of him instead of on what lay behind.

"You should almost be there!" she replied. "You have to pass through one more cavern, and then you hit another nexus with about ten different small passages. You—" The commlink suddenly went dead cutting off her last sentence.

"Kianna? Please repeat. What was that last part?" Braedon called out. He quickly wiped the sweat from his face with the sleeve of his shirt. "Raptor, see if you can get her back on the line," he said as he risked a glance behind him.

"Watch out!" Raptor yelled, causing Braedon to whip his head back around just in time to see that the floor of the cave had dropped suddenly. Unable to correct their course fast enough, they held on tightly to the Pit Climber as it fell several feet before stabilizing.

It was then that they noticed the reddish glow that came from a slight bend further up the tunnel. Along with the light was the unmistakable chattering sound of the pack of Viper Lizards.

"I don't like the looks of this," Raptor mumbled. "And what happened to the comm?"

"I noticed that we lost the signal just when we moved into this portion of the tunnel. It could be something in the rock. We have no choice. Here we go."

Braedon moved the Pit Climber forward, offering up a continuous prayer that they'd find a way out. They had barely rounded the bend when he brought the device to a stop just inside the entrance to a large cavern. For a moment, the only thing the two men could do was stare in shock.

The rectangular cavern was roughly the size of a normal city block. However, in the center, stretching from wall to wall was a giant chasm that stretched thirty feet across. Steam and hazy red light rose up from the deep fissure, leaving no doubt that lava lay below. In the light from their lantern, they could see the pack of Viper Lizards grouped together and frantically searching for some way across.

Raptor turned to face Braedon, his face grim. "I'm guessing we've only got a minute or so before the lava flow reaches this cavern, or it becomes so hot that we spontaneously combust. Do you have any idea if this thing can make that jump?"

His companion shook his head. "No, but I think we're about to find out, unless you've some other brilliant plan in mind."

"Nope. Just make sure you go fast enough and high enough to avoid the Vipers. They've got a nasty leap that can reach three or four feet into the air."

Braedon closed his eyes for several seconds and prayed. And for the first time in nineteen years, Raptor found himself joining in. *God, if you're truly real and care anything about me, help me get through this alive.*

The two men braced themselves as Braedon hit the controls that sent them four feet into the air and speeding toward the fissure. Although they didn't dare look below, they could hear the screeching of the diminutive reptiles as the gravity generators on the legs of the Pit Climber scattered them in all directions. Suddenly, Braedon altered course and sent the Pit Climber angling toward the right wall.

"What are you—" Raptor began before the realization of what Braedon had planned dawned on him. He adjusted his grip on the central pole, the sweat making his palms slip on the increasingly hot metal. He watched helplessly as the edge of the chasm grew closer and closer, the heat nearly overwhelming them as the Pit Climber rocked precariously on the shifting terrain of lizards and rocks.

With a cry of desperation, Braedon maneuvered the Pit Climber up to the wall and tilted it sideways until it was mostly vertical. With a solid surface beneath the generators, Braedon extended the rear and left legs as far as possible and pushed the device to its maximum power, launching it and its riders into the air at a forty-five-degree angle.

For several seconds, the men lost all sense of direction as they flew forward over the rift in the cavern floor. Suddenly, the front legs of the Pit Climber struck the lip of the chasm, halting its momentum. Raptor and Braedon, however, continued their forward motion. With a thud that knocked the wind out of them, they landed hard onto the ground on the far side of the fissure.

Dazed, bruised, and overcome by heat exhaustion, the two men didn't move for several minutes. Finally, by sheer will to survive, Braedon forced his protesting muscles to bring his body to a standing position. Moving slowly over to his companion, he crouched down and helped Raptor to stand. "We made it! For a minute there, I was really starting to have my doubts!"

Wincing in pain from where he had twisted his ankle slightly, Raptor forced a weary smile. "Nice flying, Ace. Although, I would've appreciated it if you could have gotten just a couple more inches of height. It looks like the Climber didn't make it."

With alarm, Braedon rapidly scanned the area for signs of the device. Risking a brief glance over the edge of the fissure, he pulled back immediately. "Wow, that's hot. Yeah, it's molten slag by now. Sorry. Nobody's perfect," Braedon said wryly.

"Yeah, and it's getting hotter. Look, that 'lava beast' that was chasing us is rounding the corner."

Just as he finished his sentence, the Viper Lizards began shrieking in panic and dropping to the ground from the heat as the flowing lava entered the cavern.

"Let's get out of here. At least we still have the lantern," Raptor commented as he limped slowly over to retrieve the glowing object. "It's a good thing they make these things durable."

Braedon had to swallow several times before he could get his dry mouth to form words. "We may be able to see, but without being able to contact the others, we still have the problem of how to determine which shaft to take."

"C'mon, we'll think of something."

Weary beyond exhaustion, the two men stumbled out of the cavern and into another tunnel. Revived slightly by the cooler temperature in the tunnel, Raptor ignored the pain in his ankle, and they forced themselves to pick up their pace. After several minutes, they finally reached the nexus of shafts.

Ten tunnels split off in various directions. Braedon and Raptor immediately ruled out the two that clearly angled downward. The other eight ranged in size from six feet across to fifteen feet. Three of them were almost completely vertical while the other five sloped upward at varying degrees.

"Kianna? Jade?" Raptor tried his commlink once again. After several seconds without a response, he swore vehemently in frustration. "Now what? Even if we randomly pick one, I'm so tired I don't have the energy to climb."

Braedon half sat, half fell onto the floor of the cavern and leaned his back up against the wall. "I agree. We've been awake over twenty-four hours, not to mention everything else we've endured. I bet you didn't wake up today expecting to be chased by *rizaks*, falling rocks, Viper Lizards, and lava!"

Raptor managed a halfhearted laugh as he plopped down next to the other. "You got that right. So how long do you think we have before the lava catches up to us again?"

Too tired to even shrug his shoulders, Braedon said, "I don't know. With the two sources of lava combining to fill that fissure, I'm guessing maybe ten or fifteen minutes."

"It's not looking too good for us, is it?"

"Nope. Let's rest for a few minutes, then we pick one and hope for the best. Agreed?"

"Agreed. If I don't fall asleep first."

"Yeah."

With their backs to the cool rock wall, the two men fought against exhaustion. Within a couple of minutes, they succumbed to their weariness and fell asleep. However, moments later, their slumber was interrupted by a loud squawking sound.

Raptor forced his heavy eyelids open, then let out a cry of surprise and alarm at the sight of a small mammalian creature clinging to his shirt and squawking as loud as it could just a few inches from his face. Startled by Raptor's reaction, Braedon awakened and looked around in a daze.

"What...what's happening?"

With the comfort of sleep cast aside by adrenaline, Raptor's brain finally recognized the small creature. Energized by excitement and hope, he picked up the *mindim* and cradled it in his hands. "Zei, you wonderful little beast! I take back all the nasty things I've ever said about you!"

The little gray creature let out an emphatic chirp in reply.

"Wait!" Braedon called out in elation as he spotted the little creature in Raptor's hands. "If she's here, that means that—"

"—that Jade sent her to lead us back!" he exclaimed, then quickly set the animal down. Letting out a final squawk, Zei leapt into the air, glided down the cavern, then flew directly to a shaft that was ten feet wide and curved upward at a more-or-less forty-five-degree angle. Filled with renewed hope, Braedon and Raptor forced their aching bodies to begin climbing the rocky shelves and rugged terrain.

Numb with weariness, the two men barely realized that a pinprick of light had appeared farther up the shaft and had begun to grow brighter with each passing second. When Raptor finally noticed it, he stopped and frowned. "Am I imagining things, or is there a light up there?"

Braedon stopped as well. "Maybe. Dim the lantern for a second."

As their own light source faded, the two companions nearly collapsed to the ground in relief at the sight of Jade piloting another Pit Climber that was moving down the sloping tunnel toward them.

11

REST

"Wait a second!" Raptor said to Jade once he and Braedon had climbed aboard the Pit Climber next to her. "I thought these things couldn't carry three people."

Jade grinned at him. "It can't handle three *men!* That's why I'm the one who came to get you. Charon alone is as heavy as you and I combined. But even the weight issue aside, it's going to be a 'cozy' ride. There's not much room on this disc for three people, so we're going to have to get close. And believe me, that's not going to be much fun for me. You two stink worse than a mud-soaked *igri!*"

Due to his extensive exhaustion, Raptor could only manage a light chuckle. "Next time, we'll try to remember to shower before getting rescued."

"See that you do," Jade chided playfully. "Alright, gents. Hang on. The sooner we get you out of here, the sooner you get to rest." With that, she activated the controls of the Pit Climber and followed Zei as the *mindim* flew ahead of them up the rocky shaft.

Finally, after more than six hours of being separated from the others, they crested the lip of the shaft and breathed a sigh of relief at the sight of the Spelunker. Even before Jade brought the Pit Climber to rest, the doors of the vehicle were flung open and their friends rushed to greet them.

"Braedon!" Catrina called out as she ran toward her husband. Overwhelmed with emotion, she nearly knocked him off his feet as she leaped into his arms and began to weep. "Thank God you're alive! I thought...I thought I'd never see you again. Please, promise you'll never leave me like that again."

Letting the couple enjoy their personal reunion, Charon, Xavier, Kianna, and the two scientists greeted and congratulated Raptor. With a smug look on his face, Charon strode up to him and gave the smaller man a brief but crushing embrace. "Man, you guys look more beat up than I do. And what took you so long?"

"Braedon and I decided to do some sightseeing and visit some friends while we were down there, of course," Raptor replied sarcastically.

"Well, next time you decide to go gallivanting on your own, try to make sure you keep your commlink on. What'd you do, break it?"

"We don't know what happened. One minute it was working fine, and then it quit. The best we can guess is that there was some kind of interference."

"That would make sense," Travis interjected. "Tartarus is full of numerous minerals and rock types that could block comm signals. When the implant relay stations were first set up, the engineers ran into all sorts of problems with—"

"Save the lecture, professor," Raptor said, cutting him off. Glancing over at Braedon and Catrina, he noticed that they had finished their private conversation and had joined the group. "I think I can speak for both of us when I say that all Braedon and I want right now is food, a shower, and some sleep. In that order!"

"Well, I'm sorry to be the bearer of bad news," Xavier said, "but showers are a little hard to come by in these here parts, and Charon ate all the food while you guys were lost."

Charon attempted to smack Xavier with the back of his hand, but having expected the retaliatory swipe, he dodged out of the way just in time and received a menacing glare instead.

Ignoring the antics of the two men, Kianna waved them toward the Spelunker. "C'mon, we've got some sandwiches and fruit waiting for you, and I think we're all ready for some shut-eye. None of us, except Xavier, have been able to sleep since you disappeared."

"Hey!" he said defensively. "I wasn't sleeping. I was just resting my eyes."

"Right," Charon harrumphed as the group began walking toward the vehicle while Jade took a few moments to fold up the Pit Climber before following. Thirty minutes later, Raptor and Braedon had washed away much of the sweat and grime from their ordeal, eaten and answered everyone's questions about what had happened. Ten minutes after that, Jade had the motion detectors set and the doors locked.

Now that Charon was no longer piloting the mechsuit, the vehicle was filled to capacity. Xavier and Charon were in the driver's and passenger's seats respectively. Braedon and the three women were in the middle, and Raptor sat in the back with the two scientists. Despite the cramped quarters, being awake for over twenty-four hours straight eventually took its toll on the group. Exhaustion quickly overcame them so that they were all sleeping soundly within minutes.

Raptor awoke to the hum of the gravity generators beneath the Spelunker as well as muffled conversation. Opening his eyes, he stared out the window for several moments before realizing that the vehicle was moving once more through the blackness of the Labyrinth. Half asleep, he could hear snippets of conversation coming from the others.

"...saw the same thing awhile back," Braedon was saying.

"...think we should check it out?" Kianna asked.

"...don't know...is it still there?"

"No. It was only there for a moment...think that perhaps something in the Labyrinth is messing with the signal, like...the commlink?"

"Probably," Braedon answered. "It's worked correctly every other time we've encountered something, right?"

"Right."

"Welcome back to the land of the living," Gunther said as he patted Raptor on the knee, causing him to miss the rest of the conversation.

"How...how long have I been asleep?"

"Well, after your ordeal, we felt that your body would need as much rest as it could get, so we gave you a little something to help you heal."

"How long have I been out?" Raptor repeated with more intensity.

"Let's see," Gunther said as he checked a chronometer. "We all fell asleep around six o'clock a.m. standard time, and it's now ten o'clock p.m."

Raptor sat up even straighter, his gaze burning into the scientist. "Are you saying I slept for fourteen hours?"

A little startled by Raptor's serious demeanor, Gunther leaned backward. "Yes."

"And today's date? Is it still February ninth?"

"Yes. Why?"

"Where are we? How far until we reach the Well?"

"Well, we would've been there already had it not been for another cave-in. We had to backtrack again. I believe Kianna and Jade said something about it being a couple more hours," Gunther said, glancing at Travis for confirmation.

"Yes, that's right," Travis said. "Why?"

Realizing that he was overreacting, Raptor suddenly came to his senses. "Sorry. I…I was just disoriented by…by too much sleep." Leaning back into the seat, he turned his head to stare out the window once more, his mind focused inward. *In two more hours, it will be the thirty-first day of Steven's prophecy— the day I'm supposed to die.*

"If it makes you feel any better," Gunther continued, causing Raptor to turn back to face him, "after everyone took a brief nap, they decided it would be better to alternate drivers so we could continue traveling. Everyone except you and Braedon, that is."

Raptor nodded and returned to staring out the window. Seeing that he was awake, Jade and Charon tried striking up a conversation. However, not feeling in the mood, he made it quite clear to the others that he just wanted to be left alone.

Another hour passed before Xavier, who was driving, suddenly slowed the Spelunker down as he stared intently out the front window.

"What in the blazes? Is that what I think it is?" Charon asked.

By now, everyone in the vehicle was staring out the window trying to see what had captured his attention. Ahead, bathed in the brilliance from the Spelunker's head lamps was the crushed remains of a mechsuit.

"Look! Over there!" Xavier said, pointing to the right. Although not quite as bright, there was still enough light from the Spelunker's side lamps to see the bleeding corpse of a large beast.

"That's a *tunrokla!*" Travis stated in awe. "I've never seen one this close!"

"And I don't think we want to get any closer," Raptor said with dread. "This looks recent. That means—"

Before Raptor could finish his sentence, a mighty roar echoed throughout the tunnel system.

"At least it sounds far away," Xavier whispered. However, his assurance did little to lessen their misgivings. Suddenly, another sound reached their ears. They instantly felt their pulses quicken. Without prompting, Xavier grabbed the steering wheel and hit the accelerator.

"What was that?" Gunther asked, his eyes wide in fear.

"That was laser and rocket fire," Charon said with a sneer.

"We've got to get out of this tunnel," Jade said as she activated the holographic map of the Labyrinth. "Xavier, take the next right."

"But...I don't understand. How could there be—"

Before Gunther could finish his sentence, Braedon interrupted with a shout, "Stop! I'm getting movement!" Immediately, Xavier hit the brakes, bringing the vehicle to a halt.

"Where?" Raptor said, leaning over the seat in front of him so he could see the display of the motion detector that Braedon held.

"I've got two medium-sized blips four hundred and fifty feet ahead and two larger ones three hundred feet down the tunnel that splits off up on the left."

Raptor studied the display for a second before responding. "I'll bet you those two ahead of us are mechs! And one of the two on the left looks about the size of a military truck. I don't know how, but the AAC have caught up to us!"

12

TUNNEL CHASE

"What do we do?" Xavier asked nervously.

"I don't know, but those mechs are just entering the cavern up ahead!" Braedon informed the group. "They'll be here in—wait a second! They're turning toward the other blips!"

Everyone in the back of the vehicle huddled around Braedon to watch the blinking lights on the screen. They held their collective breath for several seconds as they watched the mechs turn and begin moving away from the Spelunker. Suddenly, another roar echoed through the tunnels.

"They haven't found us yet!" Raptor said with excitement. "This blip is an AAC truck that's fighting against the *tunrokla*! The mechs are heading over to assist!"

"Uh oh," Braedon interjected. "We've got three more mech-sized blips coming up from behind us!"

"What do we do?" Xavier called out again, this time louder.

Raptor considered their options for a second before responding. "We follow Jade's original suggestion. Take the tunnel on the right."

"But if I go now, the mechs in the next cavern will see us!"

"Better those two than the three behind us!" Charon replied. "Now go!"

Grimacing, Xavier hit the accelerator and headed down the tunnel toward the next chamber. In the middle seat, next to Braedon, Catrina grabbed at her stomach and began to breathe heavily once again as her anxiety spiked.

"It sure would be nice if I still had my suit," Charon mumbled.

Raptor stood up and worked his way around to the middle seat. "Kianna, trade places." Without questioning, Kianna moved past him to sit in the back. Sitting down next to Jade, Raptor began to study the map of the Labyrinth. "They're gonna see us for sure the moment we come around that corner," he said. "We've got to find a way to lose them. What's in the area?"

Together, he and Jade examined the map for inspiration as Xavier piloted the Spelunker out of the tunnel and into the cavern. Raptor's interpretation of the readings from the motion detector proved to be accurate. On the far left of the cavern two hundred feet away, two mechs were rushing toward a tunnel to aid their comrades. However, the moment the lights from the Spelunker spread out in the open space, the two AAC pilots stopped and spun around to face them.

"They've spotted us!" Charon announced. "This is gonna be close!"

"They'll want us alive!" Raptor said, looking up from the map in realization.

"Sound compressors!" Charon shouted. "Everyone, cover your ears!"

"What about me?" Xavier asked in sudden alarm as he put his free left hand over his left ear. "I can't drive *and* cover both my ears!"

"Here! Charon, catch!" Kianna called out as she tossed her set of noise-cancelling earbuds toward him. He caught them and quickly handed them to Xavier, who promptly shoved them into his ears.

"They're preparing to fire!" Raptor called out. Immediately, everyone except Xavier clapped their hands over their ears and pressed themselves into the cushions of the vehicle. In an effort to avoid a direct hit, Xavier turned the wheel sharply, altering their course.

The compressed waves made their heads spin and caused them to feel light-headed. However, Xavier's last minute maneuver and their distance from the mechs prevented them from getting hit with the full brunt of the attack.

"Xavier! Watch out!" Charon shouted. Reaching over, he grabbed the wheel and jerked it to the right, causing the Spelunker to narrowly miss the left side of the tunnel entrance.

The con man shook his head in an effort to clear it. "Sorry about that," he said apologetically. "I was in such a hurry, I guess I didn't get one of the ear plugs in all the way. Those sound wave attacks are nasty!"

Everyone breathed a sigh of relief and fought to shake off the remaining effects of the attack as they left the cavern behind and barreled down the new tunnel.

"Now where?" Xavier said as he pushed the vehicle as fast as he dared. "Those mechs will be on our tail in no time, not to mention the rest of the AAC now know where we are."

"We're working on it," Raptor replied.

"That's strange," Braedon said, frowning as he stared at the motion detector. "The three mechs that were behind us suddenly stopped moving, and another blip appeared, then disappeared in the same area."

"Who cares as long as they quit moving," Charon stated.

"What about the truck?" Kianna asked.

"It appears to have finished off the *tunrokla* and is now joining the two mechs pursuing us," Raptor answered. "However, it looks like the ceiling of this tunnel is a little too low for them to use their hoverjets. They're being forced to run. That should keep them from gaining on us."

"That's risky. It could backfire on us," Jade said to Raptor.

"I know, but do you have a better idea? The AAC are sure to have most of the larger tunnels occupied."

"You're the boss. I just hope you know what you're doing."

"Don't I always," Raptor said with much less bravado than normal. "On second thought, don't answer that. Xavier, we've got a plan. Take the second left. It should slope downward."

"What's down there?" Catrina asked nervously.

"Something that'll hopefully slow down the mechs."

"If it doesn't kill us first," Jade mumbled.

Raptor shot her a dirty look and was about to say something more when Braedon interrupted the conversation. "They've entered the tunnel and are just over two hundred feet behind us. Even worse, the motion detector just picked up two more mech-sized blips coming from a tunnel to our left on an intercept course. Based on their speed, though, I think we'll get past the intersection before they arrive, but not by much."

As he finished speaking, they entered another cavern one hundred and sixty feet long and thirty feet wide. Hanging down menacingly from the ceiling were dozens of stalactites. Fortunately, only a few short stalagmites littered the floor, making it fairly easy for Xavier to maneuver.

"That other pair of mechs are coming down that tunnel over there," Braedon said, pointing to the dark opening in the left wall. Just as he finished speaking, the group could see the telltale beams of mechsuit spotlights pierce the darkness and shine into the cavern. "They're only fifty feet away!" Braedon said with urgency.

Now that they were in the much wider cavern, Xavier hit the accelerator, catapulting the vehicle across the rough terrain.

"Thirty feet!" Braedon called out as the Spelunker passed by the tunnel entrance.

"Fifteen!"

"Y'know, I could really do without the updates!" Xavier shouted. "I'm going as fast as I can already!"

"They're in the cavern! Cover your ears!" Kianna cried out.

Just then, laser fire unexpectedly flashed over the roof of their vehicle. "Lasers?" Charon said with a frown as he glanced behind them to stare at the mechs that had just entered the cavern. "What are they doing, trying to scare us with warning shots?" Even as he finished his sentence, another burst of fire flew over their heads and struck the same section of the ceiling.

Raptor's eyes grew wide as he suddenly realized the new danger. "Watch out! They're trying to bring down—"

His warning came too late as another volley of destructive energy hit the base of two of the stalactites in front of them. The large chunks of calcium salt broke off from the ceiling and plunged downward. Xavier swerved to the left, narrowly missing the one on the right. However, the one on the left struck the right side of the Spelunker, slowing their forward momentum slightly.

"That was close!" Charon breathed as Xavier regained control of the vehicle and continued their flight across the cavern. "A second later and we would've crashed right into it."

"Why aren't they using the sound wave attack?" Catrina asked in confusion.

"Because the sound compressors aren't very effective at longer ranges," Braedon explained quickly.

Seeing that their prey had escaped their first attack, the pilots in the mechsuits continued their barrage of the ceiling, sending chunks of debris flying in front of the Spelunker's path.

"Here come the others!" Travis said nervously, staring out the back window at the two mechs and personnel truck that had entered the far end of the cavern.

"C'mon! C'mon!" Xavier muttered as he pushed the Spelunker as fast as he dared in the confines of the cavern.

Larger and larger chunks of rock pummeled the vehicle as they sped toward the exit that was now less than twenty feet away. Suddenly, another loud crack of splitting salt deposits echoed throughout the chamber.

"Go, go, go!" Raptor shouted as the stalactite hanging above the exit broke free.

Everyone held their breath and prepared for impact as the new tunnel loomed before them. Behind them, the AAC pilots in their suits pressed forward, running as fast as their mechanical legs could carry them.

A loud crash hit the back section of the roof of the Spelunker, followed by the spine-jarring sound of rock scraping across metal. A split second later, the remains of the stalactite fell to the ground behind them and broke into two large chunks.

"That was even closer!" Charon stated as he examined the large dent in the ceiling just above the heads of Travis, Gunther, and Kianna. Xavier let out an enormous sigh and pried his vice-like grip off the steering wheel. Now that they were in another tunnel, he was forced to slow down to avoid hitting some of the rocky outcroppings.

"Do you think it'll slow them down at all?" Catrina asked hopefully.

In answer, she and the others glanced out the back window. After only a few seconds of stillness, the mechs reached the stalactite pieces that were blocking the path. The pilots used their suit's robotic hands to grab the pieces and fling them aside effortlessly.

"Well, I guess there's your answer," Jade said before turning to look at Raptor. "I sure hope this idea of yours works. If we have any chance of getting the Vortex set up and reversing the portals, we've gotta get these guys off our tail!"

"Yeah. Xavier, turn right at the next junction."

"You got it."

The group sat in tense silence for another minute as they traveled through the tunnel system, keenly aware that the group of jihadist militants with their arsenal of machines were always just out of range behind them. Finally, they reached the tunnel Raptor had indicated and turned. The new tunnel stretched for several hundred feet before opening into another small cavern.

The cavern was filled with an odd assortment of twisting columns that appeared to be made out of a type of clay. The only portion not covered by the columns was a path ten feet across at its widest that ran along the wall of the cavern. Flittering among the five-foot tall structures were numerous insects an inch long with wicked-looking stingers at the end of their bulbous, multi-segmented bodies.

"*This* is your idea? Mound hornets?" Xavier exclaimed, his voice laced with fear. "If I even look at one of these funny, the whole swarm will attack us!"

"I've heard they can secrete saliva that eats through stone... and metal," Travis added.

The man's careless words caused a fresh wave of panic to wash over Catrina. Immediately, her breathing quickened, and she felt her airways begin to constrict. Braedon glanced at Travis intently, causing him to realize his mistake. Embarrassed, he shrank into the cushion of his seat as he mumbled softly, "Oh. Sorry."

"I know it's risky, but it was the best plan Jade and I could come up with on short notice," Raptor said.

Again, the group held their collective breaths as Xavier moved cautiously down the path, careful not to let the Spelunker get too close to any of the nearby mounds and their diminutive caretakers.

Not wanting to disturb their driver, Braedon leaned over to show Raptor the motion detector. "They'll catch up to us in less than a minute," he whispered.

"Don't worry," he whispered back. "They won't risk shooting at us in here."

Braedon looked skeptical. "I sure hope you're right."

As predicted, the group of AAC mechs arrived a minute later and came to an immediate halt as they recognized the danger. However, after only a moment's hesitation, they began moving along the wall in single file. At only five feet wide, their suits were able to navigate the cavern at twice the speed of the cumbersome Spelunker.

"They're getting closer!" Kianna said worriedly. "We need to go faster!"

"If I do, I'll probably hit one those bug-infested columns!" Xavier called back as he wiped sweat from his brow with his sleeve.

"Here, Charon. Take this," Raptor said as he handed the Volt to the burly man.

He stared at the weapon in confusion. "Are you crazy? As much as I love using this thing, if I fire it in this cavern, the electrical currents it shoots out will stir up this nest of demon bugs!"

"Exactly!"

For a moment, everyone sat in stunned silence until a wide grin spread across Charon's features. "I always did like the way you think." Rolling down the window on the passenger side, he leaned the rifle-like weapon out the window and pointed it at the mounds nearest the mechs. "Hey, Xavier, scoot a little to the left, will ya? Any closer and I'll be able to shave with these things!"

"I'll try, but I've only got about a foot on this side as it is!"

"Better to scrape the wall then for me to bump one of the mounds."

"Both of you get ready," Raptor said as he stared at their pursuers, who were now just eighty feet behind them.

The moment the pilots of the mechsuits caught sight of the Volt, they realized the full extent of their predicament. In an effort to escape from the death trap, the mech pilots activated their hoverjets and flew as fast as they could toward the Spelunker. However, disturbed by the sudden movement of air created by the hoverjets, the mound hornets sought out the source of the disturbance and attacked.

The swarm of insects came from everywhere and quickly covered the metallic suits that had dared to invade their territory. Within seconds, the pilots lost control, causing the mechs to crash into the pillars below. On the far side of the cavern, the AAC personnel truck came into view. However, the moment it witnessed the attack from the vicious insects, the driver wisely reversed direction and fled.

Startled by the sudden movement of the hornets, Charon quickly brought the Volt back inside the Spelunker and closed the window tightly. Much to the relief of everyone inside the vehicle, the attacking insects focused solely on the mechs and left them alone. Less than a minute later, Raptor and the others left the cavern and their pursuers behind.

13

THE WELL

As they traveled deeper into the new tunnel and the motion detector showed no signs of continued pursuit, the group began to relax and breathe normal again, with the exception of Catrina. Still struggling with the aftereffects of a near panic attack, her eyes darted from window to window, searching for any signs of the mound hornets. Sitting beside her, Braedon put his arm around her shoulders and drew her close.

"It's okay, Cat. They're gone."

"How can you be so sure? What if…what if there are still some clinging to the roof where we can't see them? What if they're"—she swallowed hard before continuing—"waiting until we—"

"Can you shut her up?" Charon asked harshly. "She's ruining my sense of calm!"

Braedon paused a moment to check his triggered anger. In the ensuing silence, Kianna stepped in. "Can you blame her? It could just as easily have been us that were killed by that swarm! I'm still trying to get the images of what could've been out of my own mind. Have some compassion!"

Charon's lip curled in a sneer, and he was about to fire back a retort when Jade deflated the tension. "She's right, Charon.

Let it go. We're just all thankful you didn't have to fire the Volt."

Xavier's eyes widened, and he cocked his head to the side in agreement. "That's for sure. Seeing how those things reacted to the hoverjets, I've got a feeling they would've attacked us if you had. We dodged a laser blast this time, wouldn't you say, Raptor?"

"You could say that. Although, that was kind of my plan all along."

"What do you mean?" Xavier asked.

"I was only going to have Charon fire as an absolute last resort. I figured when the pilots saw the weapon, they'd know what we were planning and panic. That way, the hornets would be drawn to them and leave us alone. If not, then we'd wait to fire until the last second and hope we were close enough to the exit to escape the horde."

Xavier shook his head and grinned in admiration. "Nice one, boss. You're quite the sly fox, ya know."

Charon looked skeptical. "I don't know about that. Sometimes, I think he makes this stuff up after the fact just to make himself look good."

Raptor chuckled. "You could say that. Then again, don't you find it just a little coincidental that we always manage to get out of these scrapes? That's because of my superior intellect."

"Either that, or it's because Braedon's God is watching out for us."

Although Charon's comment was meant to be sarcastic, the words hit Raptor hard and seemed to suck the lightheartedness out of the atmosphere.

Catrina soon began to relax, partially due to Braedon's calm reassurances and partially due to the passage of time. The farther they traveled without incident, the more they started to settle and begin to strike up normal conversation. However, despite the lack of immediate danger, an undercurrent of tension remained as the conclusion to the journey they began a month ago drew closer with each passing minute. In addition, the ever-present possibility that the AAC could find them with every corner and juncture of the Labyrinth kept them alert and on edge.

At last, after another two hours of travel, they reached their destination.

The first signs that they were drawing close to the Well was the low rumble that reached their ears. As their brain registered the first traces of the bass frequencies, their initial thoughts were that another earthquake was beginning. However, as they continued moving without any visual signs of tremors, they began to realize that the source was coming from the massive waterfalls that lay ahead.

"It's the Well!" Gunther said excitedly. "We've made it!"

Caught up by his infectious emotions, the others leaned forward in their seats and focused their attention on the landscape that was just coming into the edge of the Spelunker's headlights. To their surprise, they began to see dim light coming from far ahead down the tunnel. As the minutes passed, the light grew larger and larger until at last, they could see where the tunnel opened up into a vast cavern. Although most of the group had seen images of the Well on holoscreens, the sheer majesty and size of it awed them into silence as they emerged from the tunnel.

The Well was, in essence, an enormous pit half a mile in diameter. Six massive waterfalls and numerous smaller waterfalls flowed from various tunnels to plunge over four hundred feet to crash mightily against the water at the bottom. Although there was always a pool of water at the bottom of the abyss, the water level remained constant. Over the two hundred years of Tartarus's existence, hundreds of expeditions have been undertaken to plumb the mysterious depths by those either desperate for answers or desperate for escape. Those that dove the furthest reported through commlinks that there were several tunnel openings that drained out of the Well. However, once the brave adventurers and their submersible machines entered one of the tunnels, their commlink connections were severed, and they were never heard from again.

Surrounding the Well were several large rocky outcroppings at varying heights, many of which stretched for several hundred feet around the perimeter and ranged between three feet and a hundred feet wide. Some of the outcroppings even ran beneath the beautiful waterfalls. Scattered around the walls of the enormous cavern were dozens of tunnels, most of which led to the rocky shelves. Others, however, ended with sheer drops.

Due to the many explorations, most of the major cities had installed lights inside the Well itself near several of the tunnels that led directly to their cities. Although there had been many discussions over the years about creating bridges over the chasm to speed up travel times between the cities, distrust and disagreements between the governing bodies of the cities prevented any construction from taking place. The lights still remained burning, indicating which tunnels led to which cities. However, none of the platforms or outcroppings were connected.

As with the rest of Tartarus, the walls of the cavern were comprised of rocks with a purplish hue that glittered when illuminated. However, like the Labyrinth itself, the stones here were much darker, creating a more foreboding atmosphere inside the Well.

The tunnel from which Raptor and the others exited led to one of the largest of the rocky shelves. The moment the Spelunker crossed the threshold and entered the cavern, Raptor and everyone else with an implant felt a jolt as their feeds returned.

"It seems that whoever installed the lights must have also set up a relay point for the implants," Travis said after a moment.

However, his comment went mostly unnoticed as everyone was fixated on their surroundings. The platform on which they now found themselves was nearly one hundred feet at its widest and stretched three hundred feet along the eastern wall of the cavern. Numerous boulders and rocks were strewn along the mostly flat surface. Near the center was a patch of discolored rock.

Once he and the others had recovered from their initial awe, Gunther pointed toward the discolored area. "That's it!" he exclaimed. "That's where the portals appear! We need to set up the Vortex and point it at that spot!"

"Raptor, we're going to be wide open out there," Charon said with concern.

Nodding, Raptor turned in his seat in order to see the two scientists behind him. "How long will it take to open the portal?"

As a response, Gunther ran through the necessary preparations aloud. "First, we need to measure the precise distance and calculate the appropriate angle. Then, we need to set up the tripod and place the Vortex onto it. Once that's complete, we need to turn it on—"

"Wait," Kianna said from where she sat next to him. "Won't that cause another....you know....more earthquakes?"

The older man patted her hand reassuringly. "Since we left Bab al-Jihad, Travis and I have been working on the Vortex mostly while Braedon and Raptor were gone. We have calibrated it now so that it won't create destructive wormholes."

"But will it open one to Earth," Raptor asked, "or will it simply stabilize an existing one?"

Gunther glanced at Travis before responding. "Frankly, we're not sure. We believe so."

"What?" Charon said in frustration. "You mean we have to sit here and *wait* until a portal appears so you can stabilize it?"

"Not...not necessarily," Travis stuttered. "We think we've figured out how to...how to open new ones."

"Yes!" Guther said with more enthusiasm. "You see, we actually made a few discoveries during our thankfully short imprisonment. We compared the three sets of data we had recorded. The first was from my work in Elysium before all this began. We then had the second set of data from the portal in Dehali. And finally, we convinced the imam to allow us to take readings from the portal in Bab al-Jihad.

"We examined the three sets of data and cross-referenced them with the different areas of Earth origin. We were then able to triangulate the reference points. Once we turn on the Vortex, we can adjust the output of gluons in order to control the amount of quarks, thus determining—"

"Skip the science lesson and get to the point," Charon growled impatiently.

"Yes, yes, I was getting to that," Gunther said. "Anyway, we are fairly confident we can make it work. Please understand that this is untested, and we've been under quite a bit of pressure lately."

"Well, not to add to your already heavy stress load," Charon said sarcastically, "but you do realize that we've got some AAC goons on our tail that could be here at any minute. So if you take too long or fail to get it right the first time, we're all either gonna die or wish we had!"

"Charon, that's enough," Raptor stated. "Seriously. You need to know when to quit. So back to the original question— how long is it gonna take?"

"Approximately twenty to thirty minutes."

"That's not what I was hoping to hear, but it'll have to work. Get started. Xavier, stop here. Everyone else, you're with me," Raptor said. "If the AAC catches up to us before Gunther and Travis have the portal open, then we have to hold them off and buy some time. It looks like there are four tunnels that lead into this area. We'll split into pairs. Braedon and Cat, Xavier and Kianna, Charon and Jade, and I'll take the smallest one by myself. One person in each group should take a motion detector. Be armed and ready for anything. Questions?"

Braedon looked around at the group and smiled wistfully. "Thank you, everyone. No matter what happens, we can rest with the knowledge that we did everything we could. The fate of every man, woman, and child in Tartarus will be decided by the events of the next hour. Let's do this not for ourselves, but for those we love."

"Nice speech, Soldier Boy," Charon said. "A little overdramatic, though. We know what's at stake. Let's just get this over with."

The group rapidly exited the Spelunker, grabbed their gear, and moved to the tunnel openings that were spaced unevenly along the western wall while Gunther and Travis began the process of measuring and setting up the Vortex weapon.

Fifteen excruciatingly long minutes passed as Gunther and Travis worked frantically and the others waited. The roar of the waterfalls became a constant drone in the background, despite its intense volume.

As minute after minute stretched by, the others began looking impatiently over at the two scientists, who appeared to be having a bit of difficulty.

"Gunther, Travis, what's going on?" Raptor asked, using his commlink in order to be heard over the crashing of water.

"Nothing," Travis replied, his voice tight from the pressure of the situation. "We just had to do some adjustments and recalculations. It might take a little longer than originally thought."

"That's just great," Raptor mumbled sarcastically, following it up with a curse. "How much longer do you—"

Before he could finish his sentence, a blip appeared at the outer edge of his motion detector's display screen. A moment later, a second, then third blip appeared. "Oh no, not yet!" Grabbing his commlink, he was just about to contact the others when Braedon's voice came over the speaker. "I've got movement on my screen!"

"Me too!"

"Uh…, same here."

This was it. The day had come. Thirty-one days since Steven's prophecy. Raptor felt his heart pounding in his chest as his anxiety spiked. Fighting against a sudden wave of panic, he swallowed hard before responding to the others. "I'm detecting movement also. This is it. The AAC have found us!"

14

THE PORTAL

"Raptor, what do we do?" Xavier asked through the commlink. "Even if we had Charon's mechsuit, we'd be sorely outgunned!"

"Not to mention they've got sound compressors," Charon chimed in. "The best we might hope for with our puny laser pistols is to discolor their paint jobs!"

For several precious seconds, Raptor wracked his brain for any kind of inspiration. *We don't have the mechsuit. We don't have any more EMP grenades. Think, Raptor! What DO you have? The Vortex—we can't use that as a weapon anymore. The Volt might do some damage, but we've only got one of those. We have three of the invisibility cloaks, but their sensors can see right through those.*

Finally, with a heaviness bred from defeat, Raptor activated his comm. "I'm sorry, everyone. I...I'm out of ideas. I can't think of a happy ending for this one. The only option is to talk our way out of it."

"Right. 'Cause that worked *sooo* well last time," Xavier said sarcastically.

Raptor's anger at his own failure flared up. "Don't forget that we wouldn't *be* in this mess in the first place if you hadn't messed up back in Dehali! None of you had to follow me. I didn't ask for this! I'm not some hero! I don't owe anything to anyone!"

Following his outburst, the others remained silent until Braedon spoke, his voice resigned but confident. "We go out fighting. They're bound to hit us with the sound compressors, so do what you can to cover your ears. Aim for any gaps in the armor."

"Sure, why not," Charon said as he positioned himself behind the right edge of the tunnel wall and raised his weapon.

Several more seconds passed before the lights of the first mechsuits came into view. In desperation, the group opened fire. The mech pilots, completely unfazed by the laser fire, continued their approach in each of the four tunnels. Once in range, the mechs raised their sound compressors and fired. Despite their best efforts to ward off the effects of the weapons, the defenders dropped one by one. Due to Kianna's noise-cancelling earbuds, Xavier was the last one standing. However, once his friends were unconscious, he raised his hands in surrender.

Raptor awakened minutes later, his insides still quivering from the effects of the sound compressors. Although his eyes were still closed, he could tell that he was bathed in bright light. Forcing his eyes open despite their protests, he winced and waited for his eyes to adjust. Slowly, he began to make sense of the large shadows that surrounded him.

"He's awake, imam."

Strong hands grabbed him and stood him up. Dizziness immediately overwhelmed him, but the soldiers held him erect until he could stand on his own. Dazed, he stared around at the ring of eight mechs that encircled him, like the giant statues of some pagan center of worship. Their searchlights were all pointed inward, their high powered beams enhancing the swirling mist from the waterfalls.

Standing in front of the mechs were a dozen AAC standard foot soldiers, each armed with a high-powered, rapid fire quad laser. The men had obviously arrived in the three military-grade hovertrucks that now rested near the wall behind the mechs. Finally, in the center of the ring of light were Raptor's friends—who were just now regaining consciousness—the Vortex weapon, and…his father.

"Rahib, you disappoint me," Imam Ahmed said as he faced Raptor. Although the mist from the waterfall had soaked everyone in the area, the imam somehow managed to retain his air of dignity and composure. However, underneath the calm exterior, Raptor could tell that the leader of the AAC was furious. "I have given you every opportunity to do the right thing. Yet you stubbornly continue to oppose me.

"And for what? By now, even *you* must realize that you are fighting against the will of Allah. You cannot run from him forever. Even in your disobedience, you have only succeeded in delaying his designs."

"You're insane," Raptor spat back. "You're confusing *your* will with *his*."

The imam smiled triumphantly. "We shall see." Turning, he looked at Gunther and Travis who were still sitting on the ground with the others. "Get them up."

Four of the nearest soldiers stepped forward, grabbed the two men by their arms, and stood them up. "You will now activate the machine and open the portals."

By way of reply, Gunther swore at the man. Travis simply looked down and remained silent.

The religious leader sighed. "You know how this ends. There is no one to rescue you this time. You will do as I command. If not, you will watch your friends die one by one. Ah, I can see in your eyes that you know I will carry out my threat."

Gunther turned nervously to look at the others for support or guidance. "Don't do it, Gunther," Braedon said. "You know what he plans to do. If you open the portal, he'll kill everyone in Tartarus that doesn't follow him and return to Earth to start a war! Better for us to die than for that to happen!"

"Brave words, *Christian*," the imam said. "You're so quick to sacrifice yourself, but let's put you in your friend's shoes. Let's see how you enjoy watching someone you care for die before your eyes. Take her!" he finished, his eyes focusing on Catrina.

"NO!" Braedon shouted as he struggled to rise. One of the guards hit him on his temple with the butt of his weapon, knocking Braedon to the ground.

"Braedon!" Catrina screamed as Taj El-Mofty dragged her forward on her knees. Seeming to enjoy himself, he took out a laser pistol and placed it against her temple.

"Jesus! Please...have mercy," Braedon cried out as he was held down. Helpless, he simply stared into the deep green eyes of his wife. "Cat..., listen to me. Place your trust in Jesus. Death is not the end. It'll be over quickly."

Tears spilled down her cheeks. Unable to speak, she simply nodded and attempted a weak smile.

"You're right, death is not the end," Imam Ahmed said. "But only the faithful will earn the favor of Allah. Not filthy infidels who despise his name. El-Mofty, kill her."

"STOP!" Gunther shouted, overcome with emotion. "I'll... I'll do it! I'm sorry, Braedon, but he's right. I can't...I can't just sit by and watch him murder all of you in cold blood. I just... can't do it!"

Imam Ahmed smiled broadly in triumph. "A wise choice. You see, *Christian*," he spoke the word like it left a foul taste in his mouth, "your God cannot save you. *I* now hold the power of life and death in my hands!" He nodded toward his general, who immediately released Catrina. She collapsed to the ground, then crawled across the rocky terrain until she fell into Braedon's arms. The two of them held one another tightly, completely shutting out the world.

"Now open the portal!"

His eyes red and puffy, Gunther stepped over to the Vortex and continued the work that had been interrupted when the Army of the Ahmed Caliphate had arrived and taken them prisoner. "It will take me several minutes to...to finish my adjustments."

The imam strode over to where the scientist stood next to the Vortex. "You have ten minutes. And know this—the only reason why I have kept you, *any* of you, alive is that I need you to do this. But if you fail or try to pretend that you can't make it work, I *will* kill all your friends while you watch, then cast their lifeless bodies into the Well. Once you've watched the last of your friends die, you'll finally join them! I have other scientists who will make it work if you don't succeed. You cannot thwart the will of Allah. You can only postpone the inevitable. Is that worth your life and the lives of your friends?"

Trapped, Gunther shook his head in defeat.

"Good. Your ten minutes starts *now!*"

"I need Travis's help if I'm going to finish in time!"

"Fine. Release the other one."

Once Gunther related the imam's threat to Travis, he finally agreed to help. Together, the two worked rapidly but thoroughly while everyone else in the cavern watched. Finally, after seven minutes, the two men turned back to face the imam.

"We believe it's ready," Gunther said.

The Muslim leader took a step forward. "Turn it on."

Gunther cast one last look at his friends, then reached down to the machine and pulled the trigger. Everyone in the room was entranced and mesmerized by the device. As on the previous two occasions, the Vortex produced a cone of particles that began to swirl in the air twenty feet in front of it. A ring of energy began to form and grow in size until it stretched to four feet in diameter. The air in the chamber seemed to crackle as the swirling circle created a rush of wind that stirred up the mist that already hung about them.

The ring of particles suddenly exploded outward, creating a wall of wind that knocked several of the soldiers off their feet. However, unlike the other times the Vortex had been used, this time, the circle grew to ten feet in diameter, then seemed to stabilize into a portal made of purplish light instead of collapsing into a black hole.

"Yes!" the imam gloated. "Well done, Gunther Lueschen. You and Mr. Butler have accomplished what no one else could. You have opened the doorway back to the birthplace of mankind. We can now return to Earth!"

15

FAMILY SECRETS

This was it—his defining moment—the moment he had been waiting for his entire life. This confirmed that he, Imam Rasul Karim Ahmed, was the Islamic messiah: the Twelfth Imam. He stared at the portal for nearly an entire minute, his eyes alight with religious zeal. At last, he tore his gaze away from the magnificent sight and turned to face his general.

"Emir Mofty, you have been my faithful right hand," Imam Ahmed said. "I now give you the honor of being the first person in Tartarus to return to Earth in over two hundred years! Step through the portal, then return immediately to report what you see."

Stunned, Taj El-Mofty swallowed nervously. "*Ya Mu'aleem*, perhaps one of the men…."

"No," Imam Ahmed said before placing a hand on El-Mofty's shoulder. "It must be someone I trust implicitly. Besides, do not so lightly cast aside the honor I am bestowing on you."

"Yes, imam. For the glory of Allah." Summoning his courage, Taj El-Mofty strode confidently toward the floating ring of purplish light.

"Return immediately," Ahmed instructed. "I want no more time wasted."

Nodding, Taj El-Mofty took a deep breath, offered up a silent prayer, then stepped into the portal and disappeared. For nearly a full minute, captor and prisoner alike stared at the portal, waiting for the man to reappear.

When the first minute had passed and he still had not returned, the imam grabbed Gunther by the collar. "What is this? What did you do? Your machine failed!"

"I...I told you that it was untested," Gunther managed to say, his teeth chattering from the cold drizzle that continued to rain down.

The Muslim leader threw Gunther to the ground in frustration. Spinning around, he faced his men. "Kill them, one at a time. Start with the women."

"Please," Gunther pleaded. "I did what you asked!"

Then, just as the soldiers moved to grab Kianna, a figure stepped out of the portal and collapsed onto the wet rocks. All eyes turned toward the newcomer. Recovering from the inter-dimensional transit, Taj El-Mofty stood to his feet and shouted exultantly in Arabic, "It works, *Ya Mu'aleem!*"

The military general rushed over to his leader and gripped him by the shoulders, his face awash in amazement. "It's so glorious! It is exactly as you described! The trees are so...so tall! And there's this brilliant blue-and-white ceiling far, far above with a blinding globe casting light everywhere! The cavern is so limitless, you can't see the walls! Everything is so...so green and full of life!"

The AAC soldiers, most of which had been born in Tartarus, glanced at each other in wonder and excitement. Even Raptor found himself momentarily forgetting about his current predicament and became caught up in the wonder of the moment.

The imam smiled triumphantly. "Yes! It is marvelous. But tell me, what took you so long to return?"

The man blanched in surprise. "What do you mean? I was there for not more than twenty seconds."

Ahmed frowned for a moment before brushing the issue aside. "It doesn't matter. What is important is that you *did* return."

Braedon and the others, unable to understand Arabic, looked to Raptor for an explanation.

"So I'm assuming it worked," Charon said.

His friend's words dispelled the sense of wonder. "Yes," Raptor said simply.

"What happens now?"

"I don't know, but I think we're about to find out."

Still wearing his victorious smile, the imam stared at the portal longingly for several seconds, then turned to face his unfinished business. Switching to English once more, he said, "You see, son? Allah's will be done."

"Allah is a figment of your deluded imagination!"

The mask of control slipped, and the imam lashed out at his son with the back of his hand. "ENOUGH! You try my patience, *boy*! I will not sit idly by and listen to you blaspheme. If you continue like this, then you will share the same fate as your infidel friends!"

"And what fate is that?" Raptor spat. "To die? Well, I'd rather die with them then live under the yoke of your oppression or that of the vindictive god you claim to serve! At least the Christian God is compassionate. I'd rather serve him than follow Allah!"

Raptor could see that his words cut his father to the core. The man shook with rage. Spinning around, the imam rushed over to the nearest soldier, snatched the rifle from his hands, and strode back to where his son stood. Raising the weapon, he pressed the tip of the barrel against Raptor's forehead.

Stunned by the sudden move, Charon and the others watched the unfolding drama with wide eyes, helpless to intervene. In contrast, Braedon and Kianna had their eyes closed and their lips moved rapidly as they prayed.

"You leave me no choice!" Raptor's father screamed, spittle flying from his mouth as veins on the side of his forehead bulged. "You are no longer my son! You have dishonored me, and you've dishonored our family!"

Raptor stood to his feet in defiance. Alert for any signs of retaliation, the two soldiers standing near him immediately grabbed his arms and restrained him. "Go ahead!" he shouted at his father, ignoring the men. "Kill me like you killed your own wife!"

His son's words hit the imam like a punch to the stomach, causing him to double over. Shocked by the revelation, Braedon and the others could only stare at their friend in sudden understanding. The piece of the puzzle they had been missing for so long finally fell into place.

The hands holding the rifle to Raptor's head began to shake. "I told you never to speak of her! She knew the consequences of her choice, yet she made the decision anyway!"

In that moment, time seemed to stop for Raptor. The memories that he had buried so many years ago came back in a mad rush. He remembered his mother's face. He remembered times of happiness with her when he was a child. He remembered her smile and her laugh. But he also remembered the numerous occasions when she tried to hide her sadness and sense of longing from him.

Then one day, she suddenly changed. In his mind's eye, he vividly saw her approach him with a beaming smile on her face. Even though he was twelve years old and nearly as tall as her, she hugged him and picked him up off his feet and told him how much she loved him. Her eyes shone with a joy he had never seen before.

But with these memories came other, darker ones. He saw his mother kneeling on the floor and weeping while his father stood over her. He had seen his father's anger many times before, but never like that. Raptor recoiled from his father and tried to run. But his father grabbed him by the arm and forced him to stay and witness what he was about to do. It was then that Raptor learned the truth that would shape his future. His mother had committed one of the worst crimes in Islam: she had become a Christian.

And the penalty for that crime was death.

From that day forward, he had turned his back on *all* religion, especially Christianity and Islam. For nineteen years, Raptor wrestled with anger and confusion. The same questions continued to plague him. His mother had known the consequences for conversion, so why did she do it? What was so important about religion that she would be willing to sacrifice herself for it? Why did she choose Jesus over her own son? The questions haunted him, and the answers always seemed just beyond reach.

Until now.

As if blinders had been removed from his eyes, all the arguments and reasoning that he had heard from Steven, Braedon, and Kianna suddenly made sense. All that Braedon had done—his selflessness, humility, and patience, especially with Catrina—made sense. And most of all, the peace that Braedon and Kianna had, and the assurance that they were forgiven had always filled Raptor with a longing he couldn't explain. Yet now he understood.

For the first time in his life, Raptor saw himself for who he truly was: a murderer, a thief, a liar, and a deceiver. All the rationalizations he had concocted over the years to justify his actions melted away, leaving his soul cold and naked. He deserved death. He deserved to be punished—to suffer. He had been running from his own sinfulness his whole life, and now it had caught up to him.

Faced with the stark reality of his sin, his mind reeled. Where then was his hope?

Atheism held no hope other than ceasing to exist. Hinduism, Buddhism, Islam, Judaism, and Mormonism were all built on following rules to earn salvation. But doing good deeds could never undo his mistakes or pay the penalty for the pain and suffering his actions had caused. He was condemned.

Suddenly, Braedon's words echoed in his mind. *"We owed a debt we couldn't pay, and he paid a debt he didn't owe."* With a jolt, Raptor finally received the answers to the questions about his mother. She had found peace and joy at last. She had been forgiven. *That* was what she and Braedon were willing to die for—not for religion—for peace, joy,…and forgiveness.

And they were willing to die for the one who gave it to them.

Then, in that moment of profound clarity, Raptor made a decision that would alter his eternal destination. Instantly, he felt the cosmic shift as new life was birthed within his soul.

Excitement and freedom mingled with the profound sense of grief he suddenly felt for his father. Choked with emotion, it took him several seconds to find his voice. "Father, I understand now! Mother was right! Don't you remember the look of joy on her face? It's true! All of it. Jesus is more than just a prophet. He truly *is* the Messiah, the Son of God!" Then, with the greatest conviction he'd ever felt in his life, he looked his father in the eye and spoke, his voice clear and firm. "I believe!"

"NOOOO!"

Overwhelmed with anguish, the self-proclaimed Twelfth Imam of the Muslim faith recoiled at the words of betrayal from his one and only son. Arching his back, he let out a wail of rage, fear, and devastation.

Then, as it had once before nineteen years ago, he felt the darkness slowly permeate his mind, body, and soul like a malicious virus, driving away every other emotion and replaced it with calm determination.

"Raptor, what are you doing?" Charon called out in confusion and alarm. Not even attempting to restrain the large man, three of the jihadist soldiers stepped closer to him as he stood to his feet, their weapons pointed directly at his head. Realizing his mistake, Charon raised his hands in the air in surrender and pleaded with his friend. "This is insane! He'll kill you! Take it back. No stupid religion is worth dying for!"

Raptor glanced at Braedon and gave him a knowing look before turning to face his longtime friend. "You're wrong, Caleb," he said. "There are some things worth dying for."

Standing unnaturally erect and emotionless, Imam Ahmed raised the weapon once more and pointed it as his son's chest. "Rahib Ahmed, by your own words you condemn yourself. I hereby renounce you forever as my son. From this day forward, your name will never again be spoken."

With grim resolve, he pulled the trigger.

16

BATTLE AT THE WELL

"RAHIB!" Charon shouted as his friend's body collapsed onto the wet stones. He looked up at Raptor's father with murderous intent, his face turning a dark red as unbridled fury coursed through him. Behind him, he could sense the soldiers tighten their grips on their weapons in preparation for a possible attack.

Like their companion, Jade and Xavier gazed at the imam with hatred, while Catrina and Kianna wept openly. Braedon continued to cradle Catrina in his arms. Several feet away standing next to the Vortex weapon, the two scientists had their heads bowed in respect.

Now that the deed was done, the imam stared at his son's body as if in a trance. A hollow ache twisted his soul. Beside him, Taj El-Mofty leaned in. "*Ya Mu'aleem,* what do we do with the others?"

Without blinking, he handed his rifle to the general. When he finally spoke, his voice was deathly cold. "Throw them into the Well."

"What?" Xavier cried out in shock. "But....but we did what you asked! You got what you--"

"Silence!" The imam growled. "You all turned him against me! I had no choice! All of you are at fault, and all of you will pay for this!"

Charon let out a feral howl of rage as he spun to attack the guards behind him. Expecting the move, one of them shot him in his right side. The stinging pain from the laser blast distracted him long enough for one of the other soldiers to strike him in the temple with the back of his weapon, knocking him unconscious.

Jade prepared for an attack of her own, but Xavier's hand on her arm made her pause. She glanced up at him and saw defeat written there. "Don't, Mingyu. It's over."

The crushed look in his eyes seemed to sap her will to fight. She realized that, like Charon's failed attempt, it would serve no purpose. Clinging to the desperate hope that another opportunity to strike might present itself, Jade postponed her attack.

The soldiers all moved into a semi-circle to stand between their prisoners and the wall of the cavern. The imam strode over to stand behind his men, his expression blank. Finally, the eight mechs also turned in order to illuminate the area.

Four of the men grabbed the unconscious form of Charon and began dragging him toward the edge of the rocky platform as their comrades forced Braedon and the others to their feet. Knowing they were marching to their deaths, the prisoners moved slowly across the wet rock.

Braedon held his wife close against his right side while Kianna held her right hand. Catrina's left hand rested on her stomach as her heightened anxiety stabbed at her gut. Her breathing was shallow and fast and her eyes were wide with terror.

"Braedon, I....I'm scared! I don't want to die!" she whispered, her eyes darting back and forth with every step.

Wincing in pain as her fingers dug into his arm, he lifted his left hand and gently turned her face toward his. "Just look at me, and me only. Focus on my eyes."

She nodded and followed his instruction. Tears spilled down her cheeks, causing Braedon to fight back his own emotions. "Cat, listen. Do you trust Jesus?"

Again, she nodded slightly as she bit her lip.

Despite their situation, Braedon felt his spirit soar. "Just accept his forgiveness, and you won't have to fear death. In a few moments, we'll be with him in heaven, and we'll never be apart again."

Catrina closed her eyes. "Jesus, please forgive me." When she opened them once more, Braedon could see that, although she was still terrified, a small sliver of peace had come over her. Holding her even tighter, he lifted his eyes and offered a prayer of thanks.

Charon began to stir as they reached the edge, now only five feet in front of them. Dizzy from the blow to the temple, he couldn't support himself and two of the guards had to prop him up. Far below, the waterfalls turned and twisted the dark pool as if impatient for the opportunity to swallow the victims.

"Throw them in!" Taj El-Mofty shouted.

Not willing to die without a fight, Jade braced herself for one last attack when, suddenly, one of the eight mechsuits turned abruptly to the right and began firing his rapid-fire laser at the cavern wall two hundred and fifty feet away. The unexpected move drew the immediate attention of everyone in the Well. Then, to the bewilderment of the captives, the other seven pilots turned and opened fire with their mechs as well. With the spotlights of the suits now focused on the wall, Braedon and the others were plunged into near complete darkness.

"What the....?" Charon mumbled in confusion.

Then, to the shock and horror of both prisoners and guards, the wall of the cavern seemed to come alive as the beams of light from the mechs illuminated hazy, distorted forms slithering rapidly along the rocky surface of the wall, the mist from the waterfalls serving to obscure their true nature. Several of the AAC guards started shouting in Arabic and pointing when, to their surprise, human-shaped forms dressed in black armor began dropping from the wall to land on the edge of the outcropping.

The truth of the situation hit the prisoners like a slap in the face: the attackers were Guardians!

Recovering their wits, Braedon, Jade and Xavier immediately took advantage of the distraction. Jade spun and kicked the nearest soldier hard in the side of his head. Even before the man hit the ground, she jabbed and elbowed a second soldier.

Beside her, Xavier threw a punch that connected with another attacker's jaw. With the man reeling from the hit, Xavier snatched the rifle out of his hands. However, before he could get the weapon aimed properly, he was forced to dive to the left to avoid a laser blast. He rolled as he hit the hard, wet stone. The moment his shoulder hit the ground, he winced in pain as he felt the wound from his previous injury tear open.

Ignoring the pain, Xavier corrected his hold on the rifle and searched for a target while Gunther, Travis, Kianna and Catrina were huddled near a small boulder barely tall enough to shield them. However, as he watched, Gunther split off from the others and made his way toward the Vortex.

Xavier had no time to wonder about Gunther's foolish action as movement from his right captured his attention. He turned to see that Charon had recovered enough to join the fight. Like a wild beast, he had charged two of the four jihadist militants that had carried him to the edge. Rage added fuel to his already impressive muscles. Grabbing their heads in his massive hands, he knocked them together with a thud that was loud enough to be heard over the rumble of the waterfalls.

As Xavier watched the melee unfold, he saw the other two guards standing several feet away behind Charon raise their weapons to fire. Knowing that his friend had no chance

against the two, Xavier fired a wild volley of shots at the attackers. Although the blaster bolts didn't hit them, the con man's
onslaught drew their attention and threw off their aim. One of
the men immediately turned toward the new threat and fired a
blast in the direction of the volley, while the other adjusted his
aim and fired at Charon. However, because of Xavier's distraction, the laser bolt merely grazed the big man's left shoulder.

Dropping to the ground to avoid the guard's shot, Xavier
focused his weapon and quickly finished off the man who had
fired at Charon. The final soldier ran for cover, hoping to avoid
another shot from Xavier. Seeing the man attempting to flee,
Charon grabbed a rifle from one of his fallen opponents and
fired after him.

"Gunther, what are you doing?" Braedon called out as the older
man sprinted toward the Vortex.

"I've got to shut it down!" Gunther yelled back. A laser blast
flew past him, missing his head by inches and causing him to
immediately drop to the ground. After a few seconds, he recovered his courage and crawled toward the machine.

It was then that Braedon saw the imam darting between
rocks and making his way toward the portal, Taj El-Mofty
and several other guards in tow. Grabbing a laser rifle from
one of the dead soldiers, Braedon brought the weapon up and
was about to fire at the imam when a body crashed into him.
The force of the blow sent him sprawling onto the ground
only a handful of feet from the edge. Spinning around, he
tried to locate the attacker but was too late. The man's fist
connected with the side of Braedon's head, stunning him.
Before he could recover, the militant leapt on top of him and

pinned him to the floor. Still struggling just to retain consciousness, Braedon knew he was in trouble.

Just as the man was about to land a killing blow with the knife he held in his hand, a large rock struck him hard in the temple. As his opponent reeled to the side from the blow, Braedon lifted his knee and shoved it into the man's back, pushing him forward and up over his head. As he landed at the edge of the precipice, his hands scrambled for purchase on the wet rock, but failed to find a way to stop his momentum. A moment later, he cried out in terror as he disappeared over the edge and plunged into the dark pool of the Well.

Still dazed, Braedon looked up in time to see Kianna and Catrina kneeling down beside him. "Are you okay?" Catrina asked.

"A bit dazed, but alive, thanks to you. If you hadn't hit him with that rock, he would've had me."

In other circumstances, Catrina would have relished the praise. However, in this case, her fear still overshadowed her other emotions. Shaking, all she could think to say was, "I'm just glad you're safe."

Together, the three of them headed back toward the relative safety of the boulder behind which Travis was still taking cover. They had almost reached it when Kianna called out. "Look!" Following her gaze, the three watched helplessly as the imam, Taj El-Mofty, and three of his men dove toward the portal. Nearby, Gunther was crawling frantically toward the Vortex weapon in a desperate attempt to shut it down.

"He's not going to make it in time!" Travis stated in defeat.

Just as the five men reached the portal, Charon appeared out of the mist running at full speed toward them. Sensing the danger at the last instant, two of the men tried to swing their weapons toward him, but they were too close to the portal. Caught in the swirl of particles, the men fell into the portal, followed an instant later by a berserking Charon.

Knowing there was nothing more he could do help Charon, Braedon returned his attention to the chaos surrounding them. The initial assault by a dozen Type I technologically altered Guardians had succeeded in drawing the fire from the eight AAC mechs. Nine of the Cyborgs were now huddled behind small boulders or taking cover in crevasses along the wall and exchanging fire with both the mechs and the AAC soldiers.

However, as he watched, Braedon suddenly realized that the Cyborgs were just the first wave of a much larger group. Far to the left of his location, flashes of blue light sprang into being on the far side of the Well and began moving toward the main battle. He knew immediately what they were, and the sight filled him with both a sense of hope and trepidation.

"What are those blue lights?" Kianna asked in concern.

"Those are ESF hoverpacks," Braedon stated.

"ESF - as in, Elysium Security Force?" Travis asked, his voice trembling.

"I'm afraid so. I used those hoverpacks before during my time with the ESF. This isn't just a small attack by Prometheus and his Guardians. This is a full out assault. They must be after the Vortex!"

17

SLAVE AND MASTER

Devyn Mathison, Governor of the city of Elysium, stood in the entrance of the cave that led from the Well to the city he governed and watched the battle unfold. As he stared through the mist toward where his Guardians and soldiers fought against the Army of the Ahmed Caliphate and their robotic suits, his eyes grew wide and shown with an almost religious zeal.

This was it—the moment he'd been waiting his whole life for!

A towering figure strode up beside him. Tearing his gaze from the battle, he glanced at the ten-foot tall Titan and the two companions that flanked him in the wide tunnel. "Ah, Prometheus. You, Cerberus, and Virus have arrived just in time to witness our victory."

The Guardian leader gazed out at the continuing carnage without speaking. After several moments, he glanced around first at the six soldiers and two other Type I Guardians that served as the governor's bodyguards before turning his attention to his master. "It isn't safe here. I told you in my briefing that you needn't come personally. Between the extra contingent of my Guardians and General Nelson's armored soldiers, we would be assured victory. It was not necessary to place yourself in harm's way, or to postpone your other important duties and responsibilities."

Mathison's handsome features twisted into a wry smile. "I appreciate your concern for my well-being, but I wouldn't miss this for anything! My other duties can wait. Did you know that my father was governor of Elysium during the War of 163?"

"Yes," Prometheus said dryly.

"I was twenty-years old at the time, and I saw how zealous and fanatical those jihadists can be. I stood by my father's side as we watched the holo feeds of them slaughtering innocents. Now, I have the chance to finish what my father started. I have the chance to make them pay for what they did. Do you really think I would pass up the chance to witness my troops mete out justice and revenge upon my enemies just so I can meet with a few wealthy politicians and business owners? Don't be absurd!"

Caught up in the excitement of his own words, Mathison was completely oblivious to the knowing glance that was exchanged between Prometheus and Cerberus. His attention was completely absorbed in the battle taking place on the other side of the Well.

"You know, Prometheus," the governor continued, "although I was initially disappointed that you failed in your mission to retrieve the Vortex and Mr. Leuschen, I have to say that—in many ways—this outcome is preferable. We get to defeat the imam and many of his soldiers, and retrieve the Vortex in one fell swoop. Your failure has turned out to be most beneficial."

Unseen by Mathison, Prometheus's black lip twisted into a sneer at the arrogant man's reprimand. Turning his gaze toward his companions, the Titan nodded. As Cerberus and Virus moved casually to stand near the other six guards, Prometheus withdrew a device from concealment and held it out toward Mathison.

"Governor, our mission wasn't a total failure," he said, his already reptilian voice turning even colder. "I had been saving this to give to you when we returned to Elysium. But since you've gone through so much effort to 'grace us with your presence' here on the battlefront, I thought this would be an appropriate time to give it to you."

Curious, Mathison turned to look at the device in confusion. "What is this?" he asked as he glanced up at the Titan. However, the moment his eyes connected with those of the genetically and technologically-altered warrior, fear shot through his heart at the malice staring back at him.

Dizziness and nausea suddenly overwhelmed him, causing him to bend over and stumble. Through a haze of confusion, Mathison heard moans and grunts from his bodyguards. As he fell to his knees, he struggled to comprehend what was happening.

Finally, as his senses adjusted, the truth slowly seeped into his consciousness. His implant feed was gone.

Stunned by the sudden turn of events, Devyn Mathison fought against his disorientation and rose to his feet to see that not only were all six of his bodyguards lying unmoving on the ground, but Prometheus, Cerberus, and the other three Cyborgs all now had their weapons pointed in his direction. For several seconds, he simply stared at his creations as his mind frantically tried to access his implant—to no avail.

With the realization that he couldn't give the command that would instantly kill the Guardians, his expression morphed from one of confusion to one of abject terror.

"What....what's the meaning of this?" Mathison cried out as he backed into the wall of the cave, seeking some escape from the monstrosities that had suddenly turned on him. "How did you...what happened to the implant feeds?"

Prometheus's half-human, half-*svith* face twisted into a smile that promised revenge as he raised his left hand to display the small device. "*This* is what happened to them. It's called an Implant Disruptor," he said slowly, relishing the look of fear in the man's eyes. "It's something the Dehali military came up with. And thanks to a trade I made with those you sent us to capture, I was able to acquire one. Don't you like it?"

Mathison's eyes grew wide as the true nature of the danger he faced struck him. "You can't....you can't kill me!" he stammered. "There's a....there's a backup system that will....trigger your kill switch if you harm me!"

Prometheus grinned sadistically, then leaned toward Mathison, his scaly face mere inches from the handsome politician's. "You may be able to convince others to believe your lies, Governor. But we've been around you far too long. We know there's no such system."

Although he was still clearly terrified, Mathison tried to put on an air of friendliness. "Come now. Surely we can work this out. What is it you want? A partnership? Your own city, perhaps? I can arrange that!"

With lightning-quick reflexes, Prometheus reached out his right, clawed hand, grasped Mathison's throat, and lifted him off the ground. The man's eyes bulged as he tried desperately to pry the Guardian's fingers away from his neck. Amused by the man's futile attempts, Prometheus smiled wickedly. Then, like a switch that had been flipped, his smile morphed into a snarl. "With you dead, Elysium will be ours! You cannot give us what we already possess!"

"Then you'll be the ruler of a dead city!"

Prometheus frowned. "Explain."

Seeing that he had the Guardian's interest at last, Mathison latched desperately onto this one hope. "If you let me live, I'll tell you what I know."

The Guardian leader tightened his grip on the man's throat, causing him to gasp. "You'll tell me now. If what you have to say is valuable, then I promise I'll let you live."

Mathison, realizing he had no choice, nodded rapidly. Once

Prometheus had loosened his grip enough, Mathison spoke. "In the last month, my scientists have confirmed that Tartarus is indeed collapsing! It won't last another day or two! *That* is why I brought the army to win back the Vortex! It's our only hope of survival now!"

Prometheus narrowed his eyes at his captive. Beside him, he could feel Cerberus shuffle nervously.

"General, perhaps Raptor and his scientist friends were right after all. This changes everything."

"Or perhaps this piece of filth is lying just to save his skin," Prometheus stated coldly.

"Please!" Mathison pleaded. "I've told you what I know! That information will save your lives! Isn't that worth a fair trade for mine?"

Prometheus was silent for several moments as he considered their situation. Finally, he returned his gaze to his prisoner. "It seems that today is the day we've *both* been waiting our whole lives for—except, only one of us is going to live to see our dreams fulfilled! My men and I are tired of being your puppets and slaves!"

The Titan slammed Mathison's body up against the cold, stone wall. Narrowing his eyes, the Guardian leader spoke, his gravelly voice filled with hatred and rancor. "You wanted to play God with the lives of others. You and your twisted scientists used our bodies as your playground. Poking, prodding, cutting and abusing us. But no longer."

Struggling to breathe, Mathison gasped for air. "Pl.... please....I'll....I'll give you....whatever you want! You promised to let me live!"

Relishing the moment, Prometheus closed his eyes and took a deep breath, as if breathing in his captive's fear. Finally, he opened them and glared at his former master. "I lied. And yes, you will give me what I want.

"I want your death."

Prometheus pulled his arm back, and, with a mighty heave, launched the man forward. The force of the throw sent Mathison's screaming body over the edge of the platform and down into the depths of the Well.

Devyn Mathison, Governor of Elysium, was dead.

For a handful of seconds, none of the Guardians moved. Finally, Prometheus turned and placed a hand on Cerberus's shoulder. "We are free."

The Hybrid's wolf-like features grinned widely back at his leader. Then, letting out the exhilaration and tension that had been building within him, Cerberus threw his head back and let out a mighty, victorious howl. After that moment of release, he refocused his attention once more on Prometheus. "You were right. Mathison couldn't help but take the bait! He had to come here himself to watch the battle!"

The Guardian leader's features were alive with energy and the lust of revenge. "The problem with having slaves is that they are often privy to their master's most hidden secrets and weaknesses. Mathison's pride became his downfall. Now, *we* are the masters!"

One of the two Cyborgs that had served as Mathison's bodyguards turned his helmeted head toward his leader. "What are your orders, General?"

Before Prometheus could respond, the ground beneath his feet shook. Looking out into the cavern housing the Well, he saw large rocks of dark stone falling from the ceiling, pelting combatants on both sides of the battle.

Although they were trained to remain calm, the Guardians all knew what the earthquake meant.

Mathison had been telling the truth.

"Cerberus, contact Specter and tell him to move in now to secure the Vortex weapon and keep the portal open,"

Prometheus commanded. "In the chaos, he should be able to reach it unchallenged. It appears we have no choice now.

"We travel to Earth!"

18

TRAPPED!

"What do we do?"

Braedon felt the weight of Kianna's question settle onto his shoulders. He quickly scanned the area to assess their options. He, Kianna, Catrina, and Travis were still huddled behind a large boulder only twenty feet from the edge of the outcropping. Gunther was lying on the ground and using the Vortex weapon for cover another twenty feet to their left. The portal still continued to swirl thirty feet in front Gunther, near the very center of the entire area. Far to the left, over two hundred feet away, the ESF soldiers and Guardians were beginning to advance toward the portal. Forty feet ahead of where Braedon and the others crouched, Jade and Xavier were now taking cover of their own behind a small boulder. However, since they were closer to the center of the outcropping, it was doing little to protect them. To the right, the AAC troops and the remaining six mechs had begun to retreat toward the entrances that led to the Labyrinth.

A nagging sense that something was amiss caused Braedon to glance back toward the ESF soldiers, this time paying closer attention to their formation. As he studied their movements, he suddenly saw it—instead of using the walls for cover, they were now pressing more toward the edge near the Well. Finally he understood, and the knowledge sent his heart racing.

They were coming for the Vortex!

"Travis, can we take the Vortex with us through the portal?" Braedon asked rapidly.

"Yes. Now that it's stabilized, we can shut it off in a way that still leaves the portal open."

"Good. Then make for the portal! It's our only chance!" Braedon shouted. Activating his implant, he opened up a TC channel to Jade and Xavier. *We're heading for the portal. The Guardians are—*

His message was cut off as his implant feed abruptly died, accompanied by the now familiar nausea and disorientation. Adding to the confusion, the explosions and laser fire briefly ceased, leaving only the sounds of the waterfalls. Next to him, Travis swayed slightly as he adjusted to the loss of the feed and the odd lull in the battle.

Kianna reached out a steadying hand, her expression filled with concern. "Are you okay? What just happened?"

"We...we just lost our...implant feeds!" Travis stammered.

"But...but that means..." Kianna began.

"Prometheus must be close," Braedon stated. "And if he's using the Implant Disruptor, then Mathison must be here as well. Now's our chance! Both sides are disoriented! That's why the fighting stopped. Let's move!"

"But what about Raptor?" Kianna asked as she glanced toward their fallen friend, whose body lay less than thirty feet to their right. "We can't just leave him here!"

Braedon quickly gauged the distances between Raptor and the AAC. "You three go help Gunther. Grab the Vortex, and jump through the portal. I'll get Jade and Xavier to help me get Raptor. We'll be right behind you. Now GO!"

Without wasting another moment, the three stood up from their hiding place, and sprinted toward Gunther. As they ran, they kept low to the ground as sporadic laser and rocket fire resumed.

Praying that the others would make it to the portal safely, Braedon raced toward Xavier and Jade. He had almost made it to them when he heard Jade shout a warning, "GET DOWN!"

Years of training to be a soldier had taught him to react instantly to instructions from commanders and companions without taking time to locate the danger. The second he saved by immediately diving to the ground spared his life. A missile, fired by one of the mechs, streaked over his head toward the opposing army, passing through the space he had just vacated.

"What are you doing?" Jade admonished as she and Xavier crawled toward him. To Braedon's surprise, he saw that, somehow, Zei had come out of hiding, found her master and was now clinging to her shoulder nervously. "I thought you were heading toward the portal?"

"I need your help getting Raptor."

"Xavier and I could have done that."

"I know. But this way, you can provide cover for Xavier and I while we carry him," Braedon said as he scanned the area. Sudden motion from behind the jihadists caught his attention. A human-sized shadow had just emerged from one of the caves, and had begun moving stealthily along the edge of the Well, clearly trying to avoid being detected by the AAC.

Braedon's momentary confusion at the sight of the hazy form slinking in the shadows quickly shifted to a deep sense of uneasiness. He'd seen firsthand what the Guardians looked like when they were camouflaged and knew it had to be one of them.

"There's a camouflaged Guardian coming from behind the AAC and moving along the edge. Try to keep an eye on him. If he gets too close, fire a warning shot or two in his direction."

"But aren't the....Guardians on *our* side?" Xavier asked breathlessly as the three of them dashed toward Raptor.

"We may have had a deal with Prometheus—" Braedon began, before ducking down momentarily as a swath of laser fire hit a nearby boulder. Once the three had resumed running, he finished his thought. "Due to the reinforcements, I'm not sure what he's got planned. If I'm guessing correctly, the ESF are trying to take control of the Vortex and the portal. Fortunately, both sides seem so intent on each other, they aren't paying much attention to us. Yet."

They finally reached their fallen comrade as Braedon finished speaking. Jade examined him quickly. When she spoke, her voice cracked with emotion. "His pulse is very faint. I'm afraid if we move him, he'll die!"

"We don't have any other choice," Braedon said as he placed his arm around Raptor and began lifting him. Together, he and Xavier got him situated and started moving as fast as they could manage toward the portal, while Jade scanned the area for signs of danger.

"Look! By the portal!" she called out.

Following her gaze, Braedon and Xavier watched as four figures carrying a rifle-sized weapon leapt into the portal and disappeared. Offering up a brief prayer of thanks, Braedon redoubled his efforts, spurred on by the knowledge that his friends were safe.

Suddenly, a tremor shook the ground beneath them, causing them to stumble. Rocks and small debris fell from the ceiling, pelting all the combatants with tiny missiles.

"Look out!"

The shout of warning coming from the ESF side of the outcropping was barely audible over the cacophony of battle and the roar of the waterfalls. Looking up, Braedon and the others watched as a large section of the cavern ceiling nearly fifty feet in diameter was broken off by the earthquake and plunged toward the Elysium forces. The Guardians scrambled to get out of the way as the ESF soldiers activated their hoverpacks to escape certain death.

The enormous rock crashed heavily against the ground like a small meteor, knocking nearly everyone from both armies onto the ground. Although many of the soldiers and Guardians were successful in evading the destruction, the resulting collision knocked several off the edge. Unlike their companions with the hoverpacks, several of the Guardians fell to their deaths.

Even more, the impact scattered and disoriented the ESF troops, giving the AAC soldiers a much needed advantage. Least affected by the earthquake, the mech pilots pressed forward. Blue flashes of light lit the area behind Braedon and the others as the hoverjets on the mechsuits flared to life, launching them forward.

"No....no....no!" Xavier cried out as one of the mechs flew over their heads and landed twenty feet in front of them near the portal, blocking their escape. Although the pilot's attention was focused on the scattered ESF troops, he certainly wouldn't ignore the approaching group for long.

"We're trapped!" Jade shouted, giving voice to some of her anger and frustration.

"We can't take down a mechsuit by ourselves!" Xavier added. "Not with these puny things," he finished, holding up his pistol for emphasis.

"We have no choice! We've got to keep going!" Braedon said. "The ESF are regrouping. If we don't—"

His voice was cut off by a new sound that could be heard coming from the northern wall of the cavern, behind the

Elysium forces. For a moment, Braedon and the others thought that the earthquake was intensifying. However, when the first of several explosions erupted from that portion of the cavern, and when those in the back of the Elysium forces began turning around, they knew it was something else.

Then, from several hundred feet away, on the northernmost outcropping, they saw the source of the sounds. Several gigantic war robots twenty-feet tall lifted slowly into the air.

"What...what are those?" Xavier asked in shock. "I didn't know the ESF had anything like that in their arsenal!"

Braedon looked at his companion, his eyes wide. "That's because they don't. Those are war machines from Dehali!"

19

THROUGH THE PORTAL

"General! Someone is stealing the Vortex weapon!"

Prometheus squinted to peer through the thin veil of mist that hung between him and the outcropping on which the battle was taking place. His enhanced vision allowed him to filter out the flashes of light, and telescope his vision. At the sight of the four non-combatants grabbing his prize, his lip curled in frustration. Looking down at the Implant Disruptor in his hand, he quickly pressed the button that would shut it off so he could communicate once more with his attack force.

Nothing happened.

"What is this?" Prometheus snarled. "Why isn't it shutting off?" In a rage, he turned and heaved the device until it crashed against the wall of the tunnel, shattering into pieces.

Still nothing happened.

"How...how is that possible?" Cerberus asked as he examined the broken remains. "How can it still be functioning?"

Prometheus frowned darkly as his anger rose to dangerous levels. "It isn't!" Swearing in frustration, he watched helplessly as the four figures disappeared into the portal.

"Follow me. Now!" With a mighty lurch, the Titan bolted toward the edge of the outcropping. Caught off guard, Cerberus,

Virus, and the remaining two Guardian bodyguards struggled to catch up with their leader.

Reaching the edge of the current platform, Prometheus used his genetically- and technologically-enhanced leg muscles to propel him into a leap that would have been impossible for a normal man. As he landed on the nearest ledge that hugged the wall of the enormous cavern, he rolled briefly to absorb the impact, then regained his footing and continued running. A second later, he saw Cerberus come up beside him running on all fours.

"General," he said between breaths, "I…I don't…understand."

Before Prometheus could respond, the sight of a large slab of ceiling falling toward his troops drew his attention. Within a handful of seconds, what appeared to be a sure victory was turning into a total defeat. And in this case, defeat would mean death.

As they ran across the wide ledge, Prometheus swore violently. "They must have placed a tracker in the device! They followed us here!"

"Who?" Cerberus asked, still confused.

Having arrived at the tip of their current ledge, Prometheus leapt once more and landed on another large outcropping. Glancing to his left, he caught sight of movement coming from the wide cave mouth along the wall. "Watch out!" He called out as he dove to his right.

Surprised by his leader's sudden warning and evasive maneuver, Cerberus nevertheless followed suit and leapt to the right. A split second later, a missile crashed into the ground where they had been standing moments before. The resulting explosion sent the two Guardians hurling toward the edge. In a desperate attempt to halt their trajectory, Prometheus and Cerberus activated their suits' ability to cling to walls. Although they failed to get a firm grip on the ground due to all the debris, their rapid actions did manage to slow them down. As their bodies tumbled over the rocky ledge, the minuscule suction cups on the arms and gloves of their armored suits managed to finally maintain a strong enough hold to arrest their descent.

Recovering quickly, the two Guardians clung to the dark stone and peered over the lip of the platform to see what had become of their companions. Several massive war machines poured out of the cave, their rockets and lasers shredding Virus and the other Cyborgs before they even knew what hit them. Pivoting, the floating tank-like robots turned and poured their deadly hail into the rear ranks of the Elysium Security Forces.

Shocked by the turn of events, Cerberus finally understood. "That's why the implant feeds didn't return! The Dehali forces are using their own Disruptors!"

"The portal is still open. If it closes, we're trapped here," Prometheus growled. Rotating his body sideways, he began crawling horizontally across the rocky wall like a spider. Hopelessly outnumbered and cut off from the rest of their forces, their only hope was stealth. With sheer determination, Cerberus turned and followed his leader. Together, the two of them crawled as fast as possible along the underside of the outcroppings toward where the portal still yawned open.

"Ready? On the count of three. One...two...three!"

The moment Braedon had finished his count, Jade sprinted toward the mech blocking the portal and he and Xavier followed behind carrying Raptor between them. The pilot of the mech seemed to ignore their approach until they drew within twenty feet. Finally, he turned the suit almost lazily toward them as if they were mere annoyances. Jade began screaming and firing her laser pistol desperately toward the ten-foot tall mechanized suit. Although her shots proved accurate, they failed to even cause a moment's hesitation from the pilot.

As if in slow motion, the mech raised its deadly weapon and pointed it at the small group, ready to finish them off. Braedon braced himself for what he knew would surely be a death blow.

Just before he could fire, the pilot of the mechsuit abruptly swiveled around and adjusted his aim toward a new, more dangerous foe. Laser fire spewed forth from the mech's arm-mounted lasers toward a Type II Guardian that was charging rapidly toward him. The lasers found their mark, striking the Hybrid several times, but failing to halt the charge. As the Guardian rapidly closed the distance between them, Braedon and the others saw that the Elysium scientists had clearly blended the man's genes with those of some kind of horned pachyderm.

Recognizing that his lasers were having little effect, the mech pilot switched tactics and prepared to launch a short-ranged rocket into his attacker. However, before he could fire, the Hybrid slammed into him.

The resulting collision sent both combatants reeling backward—straight into the swirling portal. A moment later, they had completely disappeared.

Momentarily stunned by both the fact that their way was now clear and the realization that the mech and Guardian were now on earth, the small group came to a halt.

"C'mon!" Jade shouted, urging them forward once again.

The battle continued to rage furiously all around them. The Elysium attack force, caught in a crossfire, was desperately fighting for survival. The dwindling AAC, emboldened by the sudden appearance of the Dehali army, pressed their advantage. Several jihadists, having seen their leader charge through the portal, were slowly making their way toward it, hoping to follow.

Although Braedon felt the uncertainty of diving into the unknown, he and the others didn't hesitate when they reached the edge. Taking a deep breath, Jade stepped into the swirling particles, a nervous *mindim* clinging painfully to her shoulder. Once she was gone, Braedon cast a glance at Xavier, and the two of them followed their companion.

20

CHARON'S REVENGE

The same disorientation Braedon had felt when he was dragged into Tartarus over ten years ago struck him now. For several seconds he didn't know where he was or what was happening. Brilliant light pierced his eyes, causing him to let go of Raptor's body in order to shield his face. After several moments of confusion, he slowly opened his eyes.

All around him the forest was alive with life. A gentle breeze carried the heavenly scent of flowers blooming in spring meadows. Robins, Blue Jays, and Sparrows flitted about in the tree branches above their heads, their chirps and chatterings filling the air with song. The vibrant green of flora and fauna surrounded him, contrasting with the dark rustic color and crevassed texture of the nearby maple and redwood trees.

However, he only had the briefest of moments to enjoy the scenery, for the urgency of the immediate situation struck him with the abruptness of a train crash.

He had left one battle and stepped into another.

Laser blasts flew over his head to strike the portal behind him, which continued to swirl in its silent dance. He ducked instinctively and looked toward the source of the attack. Not more than ten feet in front of him, the Type II Guardian and the mech were grappling with each other. As they fought, the mech's laser cannon spewed fire erratically, endangering everyone in the immediate area.

Next to him, he saw that Jade and Xavier were also shaking off the after-effects of the dimensional travel and discovering the danger. "C'mon! We need to find cover!" he shouted as he grabbed Raptor's arm and began dragging him behind a nearby tree to their left. Jolted into action, Xavier assisted Braedon, and within moments, the three of them were huddled together behind the trunk of the tree, scanning the area rapidly to get their bearings.

"It's...it's incredible!" Xavier breathed as he stared in amazement at the blue sky above them.

"Yes, but if you keep gawking like that, you're going to wind up dead," Jade snapped. "In case you hadn't noticed, we're in the middle of a battle!"

"Where's the Vortex!" Braedon said, his eyes searching the nearby area for signs of his friends. "We have to shut down the portal!"

Suddenly, a cry rang out from somewhere on their left. Glancing in that direction, Braedon felt his stomach lurch. Not more than sixty feet from where he stood, the forest floor ended abruptly and plunged sharply downward to a ravine full of sharp rocks and boulders. Five feet from the edge, Charon was locked in combat with Taj El-Mofty. Nearby, one of the other guards that had traveled through the portal lay unmoving on the ground. Less than a dozen feet from where the two men fought, Imam Ahmed was crawling through the grass, clutching at his injured leg.

Another cry split the air, demanding Braedon's attention. This time, he recognized the voice as belonging to his wife. Only twenty feet from where he now crouched, a little further away from Charon, he saw Catrina reeling from a backhanded blow from another jihadist soldier. She collapsed to the ground next to Travis, who was holding his arm painfully. To their right, Kianna and Gunther struggled with the last jihadist for control of the Vortex.

The sight of his wife being struck triggered in Braedon the memory of when he had rescued her from Zarrar, the abusive man who bought her as a bride. Fueled with rage, Braedon recklessly charged toward the melee and bellowed out a challenge. The jihadist instantly turned toward the new attack and drew his laser pistol from its holster. As he raised it toward Braedon, Catrina let out a cry and grabbed his arm, forcing his shot to go wild. Her distraction was all Braedon needed to close the distance. Lowering his shoulder, he tackled the man and drove him to the ground as Catrina jumped back out of the way.

Nearby, Jade had charged toward the final jihadist, who had successfully snatched the Vortex from Kianna and Gunther. Seeing the Chinese woman racing toward him, the soldier fumbled to hold onto the Vortex while simultaneously trying to draw his pistol. Realizing he wouldn't make it in time, he dropped the Vortex and braced himself for the melee attack.

To her surprise, Jade quickly discovered that the man not only towered over her and was more than twice her weight, but he also had martial arts training. He blocked her initial kick and responded with one of his own, putting her on the defensive. After exchanging several blows, she came to the realization that the fight would last longer than she'd hoped.

"Gunther! Kianna!" she shouted as she dodged another of the man's punches. "Close the portal before anyone else comes through!" The jihadist glanced toward where he had dropped the weapon and Jade knew he wanted to get to it first. Letting out a battle cry, she flew into a rapid combination of attacks aimed at keeping her opponent off balance and distracted.

The ploy worked. The soldier quickly abandoned any thought of retrieving the weapon as he was forced to focus solely on his own defense. Gunther and Kianna grabbed the Vortex and, with a glance of concern toward their friends, sprinted off toward where the mech and Hybrid Guardian were still fighting near the portal.

Braedon, having spent his rage, looked over to see that Jade was struggling against the much larger opponent. "Cat, are you and Travis okay?"

"We're fine! Go help Jade!"

Checking one last time to make sure his wife's abuser was out for the count, he bolted toward Jade. Sensing the new attack, the man's concentration faltered as he angled his body to face both opponents. His right arm blocked Braedon's first strike even as his left blocked a kick from Jade. However, as he deflected Braedon's second punch, Jade found an opening and swiped his leg out from under him. A moment later, the man lay unconscious on his back.

Knowing they were still not out of danger, Braedon glanced toward where Charon was fighting just in time to watch him land a kick against Taj El-Mofty's chest. The blow sent the man stumbling backward. He fought to regain his balance, but his momentum carried him over the edge of the ravine. With a cry of terror, Taj El-Mofty fell sixty feet to crash into the jagged rocks below.

Seeing that his companion had emerged victorious, Braedon quickly scanned the area for signs of any remaining attackers. He had barely turned his head when a startled cry of fear caused him to look back toward the imam.

Still burning with rage and malice, Charon had lifted the Muslim leader off the ground and was limping slowly toward the ravine.

"You murdered him—your own son!"

The imam struggled unsuccessfully to free himself from the monstrous hands of the infuriated man. As he struggled, he glanced continuously over his shoulder to see the edge drawing ever nearer.

"Let me go! Please! I'll…I'll give you whatever you want."

"Charon, don't do this!" Braedon called out across the uneven terrain as he stumbled toward the two men.

Ignoring Braedon, Charon reached the rocky edge and smiled cruelly into the face of the imam. "Say hello to the devil for me!"

"NOOOO!" The man screamed in panic.

Suddenly, from behind them, they heard the sounds of hoverjets activating. Turning, Braedon saw that the mech pilot had lifted both he and his Hybrid attacker into the air. Now fifteen feet off the ground, the pilot altered the angle of the jets, setting himself and the Guardian on a horizontal trajectory. A second later, he slammed the armored Hybrid up against the trunk of a tree. The resulting impact split the tree and sent it hurling toward the ground.

Straight toward Charon.

"Look out!" Jade shouted.

The snapping of the tree and Jade's warning finally broke through Charon's rage-induced fog. Turning, he saw the danger, dropped his captive, and tried to jump out the way.

"Allah, save me!!!"

With that final cry, Imam Ahmed disappeared from sight and plummeted to his death as the massive bulk of the falling tree buried Charon in a grave of leaves and branches.

Although stunned by the sudden death of one of his companions, Braedon turned immediately toward the final threat. Still hovering off the ground, the mech dropped the body of the horned Guardian, who was now either dead or unconscious.

Off to the right, Gunther held the Vortex pointed at the portal. Without waiting a moment longer, he activated it.

The swirling ring of particles that formed the portal broke formation and streamed toward the Vortex as if being sucked into a vacuum. However, once it had completely dissipated, the survivors noticed that, before dissolving, three more figures had managed to make it through.

Braedon felt his adrenaline spike as the figures stood.

Prometheus, Cerberus, and Specter had made it to Earth.

21

BATTLE FOR THE VORTEX

The instant the three Guardians appeared, the mech pilot turned to target them. However, since his store of energy for the hoverjets was nearly depleted, he was forced to return to the ground. The resultant descent threw off his aim and, instead of instantly killing Prometheus, his lasers merely tore into the Guardian's shoulder.

The attack helped to dispel the aftereffects of the portal travel, causing the Guardians to each leap into action against the new foe. Ignoring the pain from his fresh injuries, Prometheus darted toward a fallen tree on his right and took cover while Specter sprang into a series of evasive maneuvers to the left. Simultaneously, Cerberus bounded into the lower branches of a nearby tree, narrowly dodging a rocket that was sent in his direction. As the battle commenced, Gunther, Kianna, and the others all ran for cover to watch the battle between the giants unfold.

Recognizing Prometheus as the greatest threat, the mech pilot backed away from the two smaller Guardians and unleashed a swath of laser and rocket fire toward where Titan had taken cover. Pinned down, Prometheus had no choice but to go up. Gathering his strength, he launched himself into the air.

The unexpected move caught the mech pilot off guard and it took him several seconds to adjust his aim. While he did so, Cerberus leapt from one tree branch to the next in order to circle around behind the man. Catching sight of the movement, the pilot fired off a rocket toward Prometheus, and, without waiting to see if it did any damage, he turned and sent several laser blasts toward Cerberus.

With his enemy distracted, Specter took aim and managed to damage the servo units on the mechsuit's left arm with several precise blasts from his own laser pistol. Unable to keep track of all three Guardians, the pilot began to panic and fire randomly. Then, with one last mighty leap from a high tree branch, Prometheus jumped into the air and crashed down upon the head of the mech. The Titan's muscular bulk crushed the top portion of the suit and drove it into the ground, killing the pilot.

For several seconds, silence reigned in the forest as even the birds and animals were hushed by the battle. Finally, with their foe defeated, the three Guardians regrouped and turned their attention toward the spectators.

"We know you're here," Prometheus said as his eyes surveyed the area. "It will be better for you if you come out now."

"What do we do?" Jade whispered to Braedon.

"We can't take them ourselves," he replied as he looked toward where Kianna and Gunther were hidden. "Our only hope is to bargain with them like we did before." The decision made, Braedon, Jade, Catrina, and Travis stood with their hands in the air and made their way toward the Guardians. A moment later, Kianna and Gunther followed suit.

"Where's Xavier?" Jade whispered, her eyes searching the area.

Braedon frowned slightly. "I don't know. The last I saw him was when he helped me pull Raptor over to that tree," he said, glancing in that direction, which now lay behind the Guardians.

Specter and Cerberus moved to flank their leader as the companions approached. Despite the tension of the moment, Prometheus gazed at the forest with a relaxed, almost fascinated expression on his face. As Braedon and the others came to a stop, the Titan spoke, his eyes still lingering on their surroundings. "I'm impressed. It truly is a marvelous world." When he finally turned his attention toward his captives, his eyes grew cold once more. "But there will be time enough to enjoy it after we finish our business here. Open the portal. Now."

Although he didn't raise his voice even slightly, the icy way in which he spoke them sent shivers down Braedon's spine. "But...I don't understand. You told us that once you got your revenge on Mathison, you and the Guardians would stay in Tartarus."

This time, Prometheus did raise his voice as his patience grew thin. "That was before Mathison confirmed what your friends told us about the collapse of Tartarus. Seeing how it was his last attempt to save his own miserable life, I'm inclined to believe him. My men are still trapped there and caught in a crossfire, so I won't ask again. *Open the portal!*"

"Not so fast!" A trembling voice suddenly called out. "Don't move, or Prometheus gets a new hole in that ugly reptilian skull of his!"

Braedon and the others immediately shifted their attention toward where Xavier stood just fifteen feet behind the three Guardians, his laser pistol pointed at the Titan's head.

"If any of you so much as twitches, I'll pull the trigger," Xavier continued, the pistol in his hand trembling noticeably. "We don't want any trouble. Maybe....maybe we can show you how to work....how to work the Vortex and....and then you just let us go in peace. Okay? That way....no one has to get hurt."

The Guardian leader's enhanced muscles and *svith* reflexes allowed him to spin so fast that by the time Xavier was able to fire off his shots, Prometheus's head was already well out of danger. Stunned by the speed at which the Guardian moved and by the laser blast that suddenly ripped through his body, Xavier's eyes grew wide. For a moment, he remained frozen in place as his strength quickly evaporated. Then, with one last glance at his friends, he fell to the ground.

Horror rippled through the companions as the reality of what had just occurred washed over them. Catrina began to weep and buried her face in Braedon's chest. Tears fell freely down the faces of Kianna and Gunther.

Almost as quickly as Prometheus had twisted around and killed their friend, he turned back to face them, his temper flaring. "My patience with you people has reached an end. Every second I waste is another second that my men face death." Striding rapidly forward, the Guardian leader grabbed Gunther by the throat and lifted him into the air, the Vortex weapon still clutched in his hands. The others watched helplessly as their friend gasped for breath and was carried over to where the portal had first appeared. His rage barely contained, Prometheus threw the older man to the ground.

Braedon and Jade fought to control their own anger as Cerberus strode up to them, his face twisting into a malicious grin, as if hoping they would fight back. Braedon could see Jade's muscles tense as she prepared to attack. Although he knew they would die if they fought back, he nevertheless readied himself to strike.

Dropping to her knees, Kianna suddenly began to pray. Hearing the words spill from her lips, Braedon felt his own anger begin to fade. Bowing his head, he buried his face in his wife's hair and joined Kianna. This battle was beyond his control. They couldn't fight this foe physically. Immediately, he felt an inexplicable calm settle on his soul.

Gunther fumbled with the Vortex as Prometheus towered over him. The scientist's hands shook so badly he couldn't work the controls enough to adjust it properly. In frustration, Prometheus growled and backhanded the older man, causing him to drop the Vortex and fall backward onto the ground.

"You're useless! And expendable. I'll get the other one to do it. How many more of you need to die before you realize that I'm not in the mood to play games!"

Raising his right arm, he pointed his laser directly at Gunther.

Suddenly, the Guardian leader's body convulsed as multiple laser blasts tore through him. Feeling his life beginning to fade, Prometheus used what strength remained in him to turn and face his attacker. His eyes grew wide and his face registered his surprise as he realized that his killer was one of his own men.

Specter stood before him, laser pistol in hand. Then, with one final shot, the Cyborg ended the life of his leader.

Even before Prometheus's lifeless body hit the ground, Cerberus attacked. Expecting the Hybrid's charge, Specter dove to the side. Coming out of his roll into a crouch, Specter fired off several more laser blasts at his attacker, wounding Cerberus in the side. However, fueled by rage at the death of his general, the wolf-like Guardian ignored the pain, quickly altered his course, and lunged once more at Specter.

The Cyborg managed to score several more shots into the Hybrid's torso before Cerberus landed on top of him. Enraged, Cerberus tore into Specter with his clawed hands, tearing off large chunks of armor and helmet with each slash. The two rolled and grappled for several long moments before Specter managed to end the struggle with a final kill shot from his laser.

The battle for the Vortex had finally come to an end.

22

FAREWELLS

Braedon remained motionless for several seconds, his mind struggling to comprehend what had just transpired. Finally, when it was clear that there were indeed no more potential threats, he offered up a prayer of thanks and held his wife tightly.

It was over.

He turned to see that Kianna, Jade, Gunther, and Travis were also beginning to release the tension from the battle as they stared at the carnage surrounding them. As she felt her husband relax, Catrina released him and looked around in disbelief. Braedon could see in her eyes, and in the eyes of the others, a reflection of his own sense of sorrow and loss mixed with a newfound hope.

"What….what just happened?" Travis said, breaking the silence. "Why did Specter suddenly turn on the others?"

"I don't know," Braedon said. "But one thing's sure: he saved our lives. We need to find out if he's still alive and offer what help we can."

Still on edge from the battle, the group cautiously approached the bodies of the Guardians. Half expecting the Guardian leader to suddenly leap at him, Braedon slowly reached out and checked for a pulse. Everyone held their breath anxiously until finally, Braedon stepped back and announced, "He's dead."

Several feet away, Jade, who had been examining Cerberus, gave the same pronouncement. "It looks like Specter managed to get a lucky kill shot. Gunther, help me push this body off him." Despite the reassurances that the Guardians were truly dead, the older man nevertheless approached slowly, his face beginning to swell from Prometheus's blow. Together, he and Jade heaved the Hybrid off Specter. Once the body was out of the way, Jade bent down and studied the man's injuries. "He's still alive, but probably not for long."

Spurred on by Jade's words, Braedon, Catrina, Travis, and Kianna moved quickly across the forest floor to where the others awaited. "He's coming around," Gunther announced as they approached.

Braedon frowned as he studied the ripped armor and the battered body that was beneath it. Cerberus's claws had torn several holes through the thick, black material and through the man's skin as well, revealing portions of metal and wiring. The entire top right corner of the helmet had been ripped off. Underneath, they could see his blackened face and swollen eye as well as some of the exposed metal of his cybernetic implants.

Gunther crouched down next to the man. "Based on the extent of his wounds, I don't expect him to last long." Out of curiosity and the hope of bringing the man some comfort, he found the clasps that held the helmet in place and carefully removed what remained of it.

For a moment, the group stared at the handiwork of the Elysium scientists with sadness and revulsion. The man was hairless, and it was clear his scalp had been cut open in numerous places. Several inches of metal devices covered portions of his head, and the right eye, which was now blackened, had been replaced with a mechanical one.

Finally, the Guardian's left eye fluttered open. The others waited patiently while the Cyborg regained full consciousness. After nearly an entire minute, his focus came to rest on Gunther. "It is over, yes?" he said with effort. Flecks of blood touched his pale lips as he spoke.

"Yes," Gunther confirmed. "You killed Prometheus and saved our lives. But...why?"

"I couldn't stand by...and let him...hurt you."

Gunther glanced at the others to see that they all wore expression of confusion. Braedon knelt down next to the man, the pieces of the puzzle beginning to fall into place. "You followed us from Bab al-Jihad, didn't you? You were the blip that we picked up on the motion detector! Because you were using your suit's camouflage ability, it detected movement, but not enough to give a solid reading."

The Guardian nodded weakly.

"Let me guess—Prometheus had you track us while he went back to get reinforcements," Braedon said. However, to his surprise, Specter shook his head.

"No. I...I followed you on my own. Prometheus didn't give me...permission. However, once he learned...where I was, he used it...to his advantage."

Braedon frowned. "He used the Vortex as bait to lure Mathison to the Well so he could kill him. Once he was dead, he wanted to take control of the Vortex and portal himself, especially once he learned that Tartarus was really collapsing."

Specter coughed, then nodded in confirmation.

"Then why did you follow us in the first place? And why did you turn on your leader?"

It was clear to the others that it was taking a supreme effort for the man to speak, yet it was also apparent that it was important to him to do so. "I had...to make sure...you were safe. That...that you succeeded."

"Why?" Gunther asked. "I thought you always had to do as commanded. Why was it so important to you that we opened the portal?" Now that Specter's voice was unfiltered by the helmet, he felt that it sounded vaguely familiar. The hairs on the back of his neck stood up as an unsettling sensation washed over him.

He smiled weakly, a solitary tear collecting at the corner of his eye. "Because I...had to make sure that you...you would make it...safely back to...Aunt Eveleen."

Recognition hit Gunther so hard that his legs gave out, causing him to lose his crouching stance and fall onto his knees. "Erik!" he breathed as sobs wracked his body. Leaning forward, he placed his head on the dying man's chest.

Confused, but moved by the scene, the others looked to Braedon, then to Travis for an explanation. Travis, himself nearly overcome by his friend's grief, turned toward them and whispered, "Erik is his nephew who came to Tartarus with him."

Gunther raised his head to look at Erik again, his eyes red and puffy. As he spoke, he stroked the man's cheek and touched the mechanical implants on his head. "I thought you were dead! Why did you...why did you let them do this to you? Why didn't you tell me?"

Erik's face softened at his uncle's questions. "I'm sorry. I...I told you that...I needed to feel like I was...accomplishing something important. Part of the...agreement...was that I couldn't...couldn't tell my family. Becoming a Guardian means...starting over."

The sorrow on the older man's face lifted slightly as a memory surfaced. Overcome by emotion, it took him several seconds to find his voice once more. "It was...it was you, wasn't it? You were the Guardian that chased us in Elysium after Braedon and I escaped with the Vortex! You paused when you saw me, giving Steven enough time to hit you with the Volt!"

Now that his secret was revealed, Erik seemed to be fading faster and faster. But at Gunther's statement, he nodded and smiled. "When I found out it was you and what you were trying to do, I...convinced Prometheus to let me...come along to apprehend you. I also helped convince him to help you....in Bab al-Jihad." A deep, hacking cough caused his body to spasm.

When it had passed, Gunther could see that he only had moments left. Leaning close, he cupped his nephew's head in his hands. "Thank you. Thank you, Erik. You did it! You made a difference in getting us safely back to Earth!"

Taking a deep breath, Erik sighed. "Just promise me... promise me that you'll help those still...still stuck in Tartarus."

"I will."

"Give Aunt...Eveleen a hug for me. And tell Megan...I'm sorry. Tell her...I love her."

This time, Gunther was too overwhelmed to respond.

"Uncle Gun, please...please don't tell her what I became. Let her remember me...as I was. The sky...I forgot how beautiful..."

Head pillowed on the soft grass of his home soil, Erik stared into the blue sky littered with white clouds, and took his last breath.

Gunther fell across Erik's chest and sobbed, his grief more than he could bear after all the tension and terror that brought them to this moment. The others could only watch, tears streaming down their own faces as they too were reminded of all they had endured.

After several moments of respectful silence, Jade's head snapped up in sudden remembrance. "Oh no! How could I have forgotten? We have to check on Xavier and Raptor. They might still be alive!"

23

THE FIRST SIGN

Raptor opened his eyes and immediately felt his pulse quicken as he recognized his surroundings. There was no mistaking the dark-purplish hue of the rock and the claustrophobic feeling of the walls closing in.

He was back in his nightmare.

Only this time, something was different.

He didn't quite know why, but he could feel it. Something had changed.

Each time he experienced this nightmare, the images became clearer and more vivid. This time, it was almost as if he could taste the air, smell the musty odor of the tunnel. Placing a hand against the cold stone of the wall, he began walking slowly down the tunnel.

In the distance, he could see a light piercing the darkness. An overwhelming sense of futility hit him, causing him to stop. He had been here numerous times. Each time, the dragon chased him, and he ran toward the light.

The sword!

The light was coming from the magnificent sword with the ornate jewel-encrusted hilt. He remembered the pure multicolored crystalline beams that radiated from it. But he also remembered the desperation he felt at not being able to touch or wield the majestic weapon.

Despite the knowledge of what was likely to happen, he felt something else deep within urging him forward. Willing his body to move, he continued down the tunnel toward the light.

As he drew near the cavern with the sword, he stopped in confusion. In the dozens of times the nightmare had haunted him, he had always been chased by the creature. Yet now he was alone. Where was it?

A sudden desperate cry ripped through the air and pierced straight into Raptor's soul. The wail was so heart-wrenching and filled with such anguish that he felt a stabbing pain in his heart.

"Please! No! Stay away!"

Raptor felt the words like a blade twisting in his stomach. He recognized that voice—Xavier!

Racing as fast as he could down the corridor, Raptor entered the chamber with the sword and came to an immediate halt. He now understood why he hadn't been pursued. The dragon had found a different prey.

Xavier lay on the floor on his back several feet from the granite pedestal and the brilliant sword whose blade was thrust within it. Across the room, the enormous form of the black dragon crouched and prepared to pounce. The beast's blood-red eyes stared malevolently at the man, its toothy maw agape and oozing saliva.

"You are mine, Xavier Traverse," the dragon hissed, its voice sending chills through Raptor's body.

Despite Xavier's failure and inadvertent betrayal in Dehali, Raptor couldn't stand by and simply watch him die. However, when he tried to move, he quickly discovered that his body wouldn't respond. Some invisible force was preventing him from intervening. Helpless, he sought to call out, but the same unseen force had also robbed him of his voice, forcing him to be merely a spectator.

Slowly, the creature inched its way forward, stalking its prey. Xavier began to weep as he crawled backward on his elbows. Then, realizing that the sword was his only hope, he turned onto his stomach and scrambled up the pedestal, shielding his eyes from the pure brilliance of the light that emitted from the sword.

Kneeling on the smooth granite, Xavier reached out a trembling hand. The closer he came to touching the sword, the more his face reflected a fear even greater than his fear of the dragon. Terrified, his hand suddenly recoiled, as if the light from the sword had burned his flesh.

Behind him, an evil laugh issued forth from the vile serpent. Rising up, it unfurled its bat-like leathery wings. "Go ahead. Touch it!"

Turning his head, Xavier saw the forked tongue of the beast flick rapidly in and out of its mouth in anticipation. Desperate, Xavier wept uncontrollably, then reached out his hand and grasped the hilt of the sword. Immediately, he threw his head back and screamed in pain. However, as Raptor watched in horror, he realized that it wasn't because the sword was burning him. Something else was the cause of the excruciating pain.

Xavier's eyes stared upward and moved back and forth, as if he was watching dozens of scenes played out before him. For several seconds, he remained frozen in that position, his face reflecting remorse, sorrow, and grief. Finally, unable to bear it any longer, he released the hilt of the sword and fell backward off the pedestal. Sobbing uncontrollably, he curled into a ball.

Then, with a final roar of triumph, the dragon reared up to its full height and dropped down on Xavier, devouring him with one gulp.

Sickened with grief, Raptor doubled over and retched. How long he lingered in that position, he didn't know. He was suddenly jolted out of his stunned condition as another shout echoed throughout the cavern.

He looked up and felt his heart sink again. Running into the chamber from another tunnel was Charon, his head turned to peer over his shoulder. In all the years Raptor had known him, he had never seen such a look of intense terror on his friend's rugged face.

Once more, he felt the restraining force preventing him from moving or speaking. As if caught in some horrible loop, Raptor watched the same scene played out, only this time with Charon as the victim. Tears ran freely down his face as he saw his friend touch the sword and scream as images known only to Charon played out in front of his eyes before collapsing and being devoured.

"Please," Raptor said aloud, his voice having returned. "Please, no more."

His plea went unanswered as another scream drew his attention. Not wanting to look but unable to resist, he stared into the chamber again. This time, he saw his father burst out of a tunnel and into the cavern. As the dragon entered, the imam fell to the ground.

"I...I don't understand!" he cried out. "I...I was faithful! I followed the commands and kept the instructions of the Qu'ran and Hadith! Allah, I lived my life serving you."

The dragon sneered derisively. "You fool! You believed my lies because you loved the power it brought you. Touch the sword and learn the truth!"

The imam winced as the purity of the sword's light pierced his eyes. "No..." he moaned. "I can't!"

"Yes!" it hissed gleefully. "You must!"

Wailing uncontrollably, the imam climbed up the pedestal. His eyes grew wide, and his movements were as one being compelled to press forward. At last, his hand touched the hilt. Despite all that his father had done, it still grieved Raptor to see *the man scream in horror and pain. Moments later, it was over, the dragon having fed once more.*

Numb from all he had witnessed, it took Raptor a moment to realize the chamber was empty. The dragon was gone.

Suddenly, he heard it again. Fear gripped his heart as the certainty of what was about to occur struck him.

It was his turn. The dragon was coming for him.

He understood how Xavier, Charon, and his father had felt. He knew the dragon brought certain death, yet he also didn't want to face the brilliance and purity of the sword, much less the unknown vision that awaited him when he touched it. Yet like the others, he found his feet moving as if he was being drawn toward it.

Raptor reached the pedestal just as the dragon entered the chamber. "Why do you run? You are mine! You have been my property your whole adult life. There is no escape for you!"

Was it true? Was there really no escape from the dragon? But if so, then why was there a sword? Surely, someone *must* be able to wield it.

Fighting against his despair and the brightness of the light coming from the weapon, Raptor turned to stare at the magnificent blade. The rainbow of colors created by the beautiful jewels called out to him. Suddenly, an odd sense of peace came over him. Closing his eyes, he took a deep breath and grabbed the hilt.

Instantly, images from his life began flashing before his eyes. He saw himself as a child, bullying others, stealing, and lying to his mother. He watched as he ruined the lives of women by taking that which wasn't his. He was unable to look away as he murdered men for wealth and pleasure. Suddenly, with a clarity that dispelled all rationalizations and excuses, he looked into the depths of his black soul and saw every sinful thing he had ever done.

He began to scream from the wickedness of his own heart, unable to endure the naked truth. Then, just as he felt his sanity slipping, the images began to be covered by droplets of red liquid. One by one, the droplets merged to become a trickle, a stream, and then a river—a river of blood that blotted out the horror of his sin.

Stunned, Rahib Ahmed looked down to see that he was now clothed in a white robe and the sword was still in his hand. Turning, he looked at the dragon. Only this time, he saw fear in the villain's red eyes.

"No!" the beast shouted as it began to shrink away from him. "You...you were mine!"

Rahib spoke, his voice imbued with a strength that was not his own. "I may have been yours, but now I belong to another. He bought my soul and ransomed me with the blood of his only Son!" Brandishing the sword in front of him, he jumped off the pedestal and advanced toward his enemy. "You've lost! Go back to the abyss from which you came and haunt me no more!"

Breaking into a run, Rahib quickly closed the distance between himself and the retreating creature. With a shout of triumph, he plunged the sword deep into the wicked fiend. The dragon howled with pain as the blade pierced its scaly hide. Rahib withdrew the weapon and prepared to strike again. However, having felt the sting of the mighty sword, the serpent twisted its lithe body around and fled down one of the tunnels.

He stood for several moments, amazed at what had just transpired. In awe, he stared at the ancient weapon he held in his hand that had the power to banish the beast.

"Rahib."

He spun around at the sound of the voice. At first, he didn't recognize the white-robed figure walking toward him, though there was something familiar in the way the person said his name.

"Who are you?"

The figure was an Arab woman who appeared to be in her mid-twenties. As she drew closer, Raptor felt his knees weaken, and he collapsed to the ground in shock. He recognized her soft, brown eyes and beautiful black hair, but she was filled with so much grace and joy that he barely recognized her.

"Mother?"

"Yes, my son," she said with a smile so warm that is seemed to chase away the darkness of the tunnel. The sword slipped from his hand as tears that had been held back since the day she died poured like a waterfall down his cheeks. Kneeling next to him, she cupped his face in her gentle hands.

At her touch, he closed his eyes. Like a little child, he wrapped his arms around her and wept with joy. For the first time in nineteen years, Nadya Ahmed held her son. Then, like the flip of a switch, Raptor pulled back from her and let out a hearty laugh. Caught up in his joy, Nadya found herself laughing with him.

"How...how is this possible?" Rahib asked finally. "You...you look so...young! Where are we?"

His mother laughed again. "All your questions will be answered in time. Come. Walk with me."

She took his hand, and together they began walking. It was only then that Rahib realized they were no longer in the dark tunnels of the Labyrinth, but were now walking in a beautiful garden with a crystal blue sky overhead.

"Mother, what's happening?"

Nadya's smile wilted slightly. "You are passing from one life to another. Even now, you are taking your last breaths in the Shadowlands and will be entering your new life."

Rahib pondered her words for several moments. "Then I'm really dead. I...I failed. Steven's prophecy was wrong."

"Why do you say that?"

"I knew immediately when he spoke the prophecy that the first section was about you. But...he also said that 'tens of thousands

will live or perish by your choices' and that my 'fate is bound to theirs.' I failed to help the people of Tartarus return to Earth. If my fate is bound to theirs, then they'll die also."

His mother shook her head patiently. "My son, as with many prophecies, the fulfillment of them is often quite different than the way we perceive them initially. The words say they will live or perish 'by your choices.' Since you chose to help Braedon and Gunther seek out a way to open the portals, then you set the people of Tartarus on that same path. Their fate was bound to yours in the sense that, had you chosen not to help, Gunther and Braedon would not have succeeded, and the way back to Earth would still be closed."

His mother's words eased his mind, but then he frowned as a new thought occurred. "But what about the next lines? 'Only by opening the door to a new life will your own be saved. You must seek out truth, for only the truth will set you free.' I thought that meant the only way I could live was by opening the portals, leading to a new life on Earth. Yet I didn't live."

"Again, you misread the prophecy," Nadya explained. "You opened the door to a new life by accepting Jesus as your savior. He is the door, and the 'new life' is your eternal life with him. That is how your life was 'saved'. You did seek out the truth, and it has set you free—from the bondage of sin."

Rahib felt as if a veil had been lifted, and for the first time, he was seeing reality clearly. "What happened back in the chamber with the sword and the dragon?"

"That was the fulfillment of the First Sign that Steven gave to you when he spoke the prophecy. God allowed you to be plagued with the nightmare of the dragon to keep you seeking him. Now at the end of your life, God showed you the conclusion of that vision. The sword on the pedestal was the sword of the spirit, which is the Word of God. It acts like a mirror, causing us to see ourselves as God himself does." Her expression fell as she continued. "*Unfortunately, when the truth of our sinful state is revealed to the unrepentant, such as your father and your friends, it drives them mad. Only you were able to wield the sword and smite the enemy because your sins had been cast away by the blood of Jesus.*"

"*But what about Xavier?*" Rahib asked. "*He was a Christian. Why couldn't he wield the sword?*"

"*You already know the answer to that,*" Nadya said. "*You recognized long ago the difference between Xavier's faith and the faith of Steven, Kianna, and Braedon. Their faith came from the heart and their actions reflected their conviction. But Xavier was a Christian in name only. In his heart, he had never repented or truly accepted the free gift of salvation. He bought into one of the world's greatest lies—that all religions lead to God. But no matter how sincerely one believes a lie and repeats it, it will never change it into a truth.*"

Rahib nodded and was silent for several moments as he absorbed her words. "*I only wish I had known the truth sooner. Maybe I could have convinced Charon, Xavier, and…and my father of the truth. Then perhaps they could have been saved as well.*"

"*Every decision a person makes in life brings him closer to God or pushes him farther away. Your father and friends had numerous opportunities to accept the truth, but they hardened their hearts. I tried to share the truth with your father, but…he wouldn't listen.*"

Her words brought back to his mind the pain he felt when he lost her. And with that pain came more questions. "*I now believe in God, but I still don't understand why he allowed you to be taken away from me. So much of the pain and suffering in my life could have been avoided if only you had lived. You could've taught me about Jesus, and…I wouldn't have made so many mistakes.*"

His mother placed a hand on his arm. "*Son, there is so much you don't understand. God's ways are not our ways, and we don't* know what 'would have happened' in any situation. The main point to remember is that the most important thing in God's economy is a lost soul that finds his or her way home. Because of that, God will do whatever it takes to set that person on a path that will lead them to the truth. That path often requires them to endure suffering and pain, and it is often because of that suffering and pain that they find their way to the Lord.

"And in your case," she continued, "your loss set you on a journey that not only led you to Jesus, but also made it possible for tens of thousands of people to escape from Tartarus."

"—If Braedon and Gunther succeed."

"That's true. But it was your choices and actions that at least have given them a chance. Which brings up another point—God has a will for our lives, but he has also given us free will. Too often, we abuse that privilege and make choices that are in opposition to his will. When that happens, suffering often follows.

"When you were three-years old, we were sitting by an open fire, and I told you not to touch it. You were so stubborn that you kept reaching for it, despite several warnings from me. Finally, I let you have your way and you burned your finger. In the same way, we often suffer because of our own foolish mistakes or the mistakes of others.

"You see, your father made a terrible choice, and you and your sister had to suffer the consequences. But even then, God, in his infinite wisdom, used that tragedy to set you on a path that eventually led to your salvation."

His mother suddenly stopped walking and turned toward him, her face a mixture of sadness and joy. "It's over now, son. Your transition is complete. Your life in Tartarus is now nothing more than a bad memory. Now prepare for real life! It's time to go home."

Rahib felt excitement course through him at the wonders he was about to behold. He looked at his mother and smiled broadly. "Lead the way!"

She smiled back. "That privilege belongs to another. Son, let me introduce you to someone who's been waiting all your life to meet you."

Rahib followed her gaze to see a man walking toward them, his nail-pierced hands outstretched to embrace his prodigal son.

24

HOME

Braedon and Jade moved quickly to check on their fallen friends, only to have their fears confirmed—Raptor and Xavier were dead.

Despite the need to grieve the loss of their companions, they knew that they had to secure the area and make sure none of the other combatants would regain consciousness to attack once more. Over the next several minutes, the group rushed around the area to examine each of the bodies for signs of life. During their search, they discovered that two of the jihadist soldiers were still alive, but unconscious. They removed their weapons and bound their hands with strips of cloth to prevent them from causing any further trouble. When they had at last confirmed that the mech pilot was also dead, they knew it was truly over.

Now that the anxiety from the battle had faded, Jade, Kianna, and Travis, who'd lived their entire lives in Tartarus, began to gaze at their surroundings with amazement. Their expressions of awe and wonder actually succeeded in breaking through the dark cloud of grief that had settled over the group, causing Braedon and Catrina to smile for the first time in a long while.

"Welcome to Earth!" Braedon stated triumphantly. "You three look like kids who just stepped into Willy Wonka's Chocolate Factory!"

The three Tartarus natives tore their gazes away from the amazing sights around them and stared at him in confusion. "Wolly Winka's what?" Kianna muttered.

Catrina and Braedon chuckled lightly while the others, still caught up in the awe of what they were seeing, strode over to the trees and plants and began to touch them. "These trees are so different from the ones that grow in Tartarus!" Travis said as his hand moved up and down the trunk to take in the rough texture.

A sudden commotion from above caught everyone's attention. Zei was leaping about wildly from branch to branch chasing birds, squirrels and any other moving critter she could find. The group laughed once more, the small mammal's antics working as an antidote to drive away some of the heaviness of recent events.

With the initial sense of wonderment beginning to fade, Travis turned toward Braedon. "I'm truly amazed at all this, and I don't mean to ruin the moment for the three of you, but some of us still have family back in Tartarus. We have to go back!"

At his words, the smile evaporated from Catrina's face and she shrank back against Braedon. "I...I can't go back there. I can't—"

"It's okay, Cat," Braedon said calmly. "No one expects you to."

Knowing that there was still work to be done, Gunther stood up and walked over to rejoin the group, his face pale and tear-streaked. After Kianna and Catrina had each taken turns hugging him, Braedon and Travis placed a comforting hand on his shoulder.

"Thank you. All of you," Gunther said at last, fighting to control the quiver in his voice. "I heard you talking about going back and wanted to do what I could to help."

"Yes," Braedon said simply. "You told us before that you can now control the portals, is that right?"

"Yes, we believe so."

"Good, then the only question is—who else is coming with me?"

Catrina pulled back from him. "What? You can't go back! Please, Braedon. Don't leave me again!"

Braedon cupped her cheek with his left hand and caressed her smooth skin. "I have to, Cat. Those people will die if we don't go back. They need us."

"But....why can't Travis and the others go if they want to? Why do you have to go?"

"Because they need me. I need to finish what I started. I have to honor Raptor, Steven, and everyone else who has sacrificed to help us. Besides, we're only going to the Welcome Centers, not to the Well."

She put her head on his chest for comfort. "Promise me you'll come back."

"I promise."

Gunther came up beside them and placed a hand on Braedon's shoulder. As he spoke, his gaze bounced between Travis and Braedon before falling toward the ground in shame. "I...I can't do it either. I can't go back there. I've already been away far too long."

"It's okay, Gunther," Kianna said. "We don't blame you."

"But you should blame me," he said, his voice low. "After all, none of this would've happened if it weren't for me."

The others stared at him in confusion. "Don't be so hard on yourself," Travis said with a chuckle. "It's not like you created the portals in the first place."

When Gunther's expression of guilt didn't lift, Travis felt his stomach drop. "You...you didn't, did you?"

Gunther stared at the ground as he spoke, his voice barely audible. "Not directly. I had a bad feeling it would be the case, but I wasn't sure—that is, until we got the readings from the Dehali portal. I then realized that my worst fears were true."

"What do you mean?" Kianna asked, her voice going cold. "What fears?"

The gray-haired, balding man seemed to age before their eyes as the weight of his secret bore down on him. "I was a particle physicist here on Earth. That's why they immediately put me to work on the Vortex when I arrived in Elysium. But when I was here, I was working with other scientists at the European Organization for Nuclear Research, known as CERN. I was honored to be chosen to gain access to the Large Hadron Collider in their accelerator complex beneath the France-Switzerland border. The LHC is the most powerful particle accelerator in the world!"

The group continued to stare at him in confusion. "What does this have to do with the portals?" Jade asked.

"Well, when I studied the data from the portal in Dehali, I recognized the patterns of composite particles. All the data was almost exactly what I had seen during my time at CERN. Although I realized what this meant, I wasn't certain of it until I was able to check the data from the portal in Bab al-Jihad. It was then that my theory was confirmed."

He paused for a moment before continuing. "The LHC was first activated on September 10, 2008. The portals began appearing just months after that time."

Everyone in the group was frozen in place with their eyes wide as they understood the truth.

"Yes," Gunther nodded. "The Large Hadron Collider opened the portals to Tartarus. The scientists believed it would be safe, but it ended up weakening the fabric of space and time, opening portals to Tartarus in remote areas."

"Why remote areas? How come they didn't open up in cities?" Kianna asked.

Gunther shrugged. "My guess would be that all the electricity and concrete interfered with the wormholes."

"But exactly where is Tartarus?" Catrina asked. "Is it deep underground on Earth, or another planet, or...something else?"

Travis shook his head. "We don't know for sure. We may never know. I have speculated that perhaps, because the collider is housed almost six hundred feet underground, it opened up portals from the surface to caverns deep in the Earth's crust. But then again, that wouldn't explain the unknown metals or creatures we discovered there."

"Besides," Gunther interjected, "the readings from the portals seemed to indicate a wormhole at least large enough to travel to another planet. If Tartarus were located somewhere on Earth, the wormhole should have been miniscule. However, since we're dealing with theoretical physics here, we can't be one hundred percent sure."

"For all we know, it may have even opened up a portal to another dimension," Travis offered. He looked like he was going to say more, but just as he was opening his mouth, another thought took its place. "Wait a minute! You said the collider was turned on in 2008. That's the same year the First Colony arrived in Tartarus!"

"Exactly," Gunther confirmed.

"If all that's true, then why is it when newcomers arrive in Tartarus, they are projected forward in time?" Travis asked. "I mean, Gunther, when you were dragged into Tartarus, you said you were from 2047, yet you arrived in 2210. That means you traveled one hundred sixty years into the future!"

"True, but I also did some calculations on that. It appears that time passes at a different rate on Earth than it does in Tartarus."

"What do you mean?" Braedon asked.

"As I already noted, the LHC was turned on in 2008," Gunther explained. "That means that the First Colony began in the same year. However, if you look at the data from those who arrive from Earth, you will find a clear correlation. In essence, the ratio of Tartarus time to Earth time is five-to-one."

"You mean, for every five minutes that passes in Tartarus, only one minute passes on Earth?" Kianna asked incredulously.

"Yes. If you remember, Taj El-Mofty told the imam that he was only on Earth for twenty seconds, yet for us, a minute and a half passed."

"Amazing," Kianna muttered. "So, what does it all mean?"

"I'm not certain if the effect works in reverse, but...." Gunther paused as he did a quick calculation, "it could mean that we've arrived back on earth not in 2210, but rather in 2048. Although I have lived five years in Tartarus, only one year has passed here on Earth."

"That would mean...Cat, we've only been gone two years, even though we're ten years older!" Braedon exclaimed in shock.

"Wait a second," Travis said in sudden realization. "If this is true, then we can't waste any more time! We have to return to Tartarus now! The earthquakes were already starting to increase in frequency. For those in Tartarus, we've already been gone for a half hour!"

"You're right," Braedon said. "Travis, do you know how to adjust the Vortex to change locations within Tartarus?"

"Yes."

"Good. Look, I know that we need to return quickly, but we need to do something with the bodies. We don't want the first sight the refugees from Tartarus see when they arrive to be a bunch of dead people. Quickly, let's put them at the bottom of that small incline over there, then we'll cover them with branches and whatever else we can find until we can take care of them properly."

Working rapidly, the men moved the bodies to the indicated spot while Kianna and Catrina found something to cover them with. In less than ten minutes, they had finished their task and had returned to the clearing in which they had arrived. "Gunther, Cat, as soon as we're gone, I want you to scout around the area and see if you can find some help. Try to locate some high ground and look for roads, houses…anything. Maybe even climb a tree if you have to. Once we open the portal, there's going to be a steady stream of people coming through that will need direction."

"We'll do what we can," Gunther promised.

Taking Catrina in his arms, Braedon kissed her briefly. "We'll be back soon. In fact, if Gunther's right about the time difference, then we should be back before you know it."

"Please be careful."

"I will. Travis, fire it up. Let's go rescue your families!"

25

A NEW LIFE

Gunther stared out the window of the building, his eyes searching the night sky. Although he had missed the beauty of Earth, his raging emotions overpowered the splendor of the city lights.

He was going to see his wife!

Despite his excitement, a host of other feelings vied for dominance within him. He couldn't wait to see Eveleen. His stomach did flips at the thought of their reunion. Yet, an irrational sense of worry haunted him. Although he had spent five long years in Tartarus, the time difference between worlds meant that only one year had passed on Earth. How much had changed?

Added to these feelings was the dread he felt at having to tell Erik's fiancé, Megan, that he had died in Tartarus. He struggled with his own sense of failure at not protecting his nephew, and for taking him on that fateful trip into the woods that led to them being pulled into the portal in the first place.

Then, there was the knowledge that his research at CERN had opened the portals back in 2008, ripping so many lives apart. What would he do with that knowledge now? How would he convince the world that the particle accelerator had to be shut down? Regardless of the outcome, he knew he would have to speak out and do what he could to get them to realize the truth.

On top of that, he felt the loss of Raptor, Charon, and Xavier. Although he had only met them a month ago, the trials and dangers they had faced had brought a comradery that wasn't easily broken. He also felt the weight of knowing that they risked their lives for him, which was a debt he could never repay.

He carried all this in his spirit, longing for some release. He needed some way to remove this weight—someone to lift his burdens…

The memory of the imam preparing to strike down Braedon in Bab al-Jihad suddenly came to his mind. He remembered the look of peace on the man's face. *How can one be so at peace when facing certain death?* Gunther wondered. *It was the same look that Raptor had just before he died. Perhaps…perhaps I should have a conversation with Braedon. Perhaps he can show me how to have that kind of peace.*

The audio from the local evening news caught his attention, brushing his thoughts aside. He glanced over at the wall mounted projector that was currently showing video footage of the refugees from Tartarus from all over the globe.

"Unless you've been living in a cave these past several days, you've no doubt heard about the refugees that mysteriously appeared here in Wisconsin, and in five other locations around the world."

Beside the news anchor at his desk, one of the female anchors gave him a sideways look at his choice of words. "Really, John? That was a terrible pun," she chided good-naturedly.

Smiling, the man continued. "Now, the governments of Sudan, China, India, Iran, Spain, and the U.S. are working overtime to figure out what to do with the tens of thousands of people, many carrying nothing more than the shirts on their backs, that suddenly appeared inside their borders. We now go live to our correspondent, Sydney King, who is on location with the refugees here in Wisconsin. Sydney?"

"Thank you, John," she said as the screen showed the dark-haired reporter dressed in a sharp business suit. "When the first refugees began arriving from Tartarus, many were carrying suitcases, boxes full of valuable items, and many other personal effects. However, after the first day, government officials from each of the affected cities began reporting that some of the refugees were arriving on Earth with little or no possessions. Many of the families that showed up on the second day told stories of massive earthquakes and destruction. Then, at precisely five-forty-three p.m., all six of the portals closed simultaneously. The very last refugees to pass through described scenes of mass hysteria as the entire world of Tartarus collapsed."

The images on the screen switched from the reporter to showing video footage of the refugees. However, instead of images of large groups, the news editor chose to focus on individuals. When the video changed to show citizens from Bab al-Jihad, Gunther felt his heart skip a beat from joy as he caught a brief glimpse of Raptor's sister, Zahra, and her husband. It was several moments before he turned his attention back to the voice of the reporter.

"While it has been confirmed that tens of thousands of people escaped the doomed world, hundreds of thousands more perished. Sadly, the stories that have been told mirror those from other tragedies, such as the Titanic. The warnings were given with enough time for everyone to escape, yet many didn't act on those warnings until it was too late.

"As of now, the United Nations has begun working directly with the governments of the six host countries to assist in the relocation of the refugees. However, this is proving to be a very difficult and complicated task. Those who were pulled into Tartarus within the last ten years or so will be allowed to return home. But for others, things aren't so easy.

"Now that the authorities have had a chance to interview more of the refugees, fascinating details are emerging in this developing story. Just today, the government released a statement that they have learned that time passed at a quicker rate for those trapped in Tartarus! For every year that passed on earth, five years passed there. It may sound like something out of a science-fiction novel, but there have even been recorded instances of entire generations living their lives in Tartarus. This means that, for some of the earliest cases of disappearances, those who are returning are the great-great-grandchildren of the person who went missing! For these refugees, they have no place—no country—to even call their own."

"Wow. That's simply hard to wrap my head around," the original anchor said as she finished her report. "So, with all this going on, what's happening with the local refugees? Where are they staying?"

"Well, until everything gets sorted out, the citizens of the city of Elysium that arrived in the north woods have been transported to various schools and government buildings where they will be housed temporarily," Sydney answered.

"Who's taking care of their medical needs?" the female co-host asked, her brow furrowed in concern.

"In addition to the local workers, medical staff and volunteers from all over the region have come to help treat the wounded, and administer physicals."

"Thank you, Sydney," the anchor said. Then, turning to the camera, he added, "We'll keep you up to date on the latest developments as this historic situation continues to unfold."

"It'll be your turn next, Gunther," Braedon said as he walked over and sat down next to his friend, pulling his attention away from the news report. Noting the other man's disturbed expression, he frowned slightly. "Are you okay? Are you nervous about talking to Eveleen?"

"Yes, some. But it's more than that," Gunther answered, his gaze never leaving the window. "It's just...so much has happened. I was just watching the news and they were talking about how many of the people from Tartarus have no place to go. Travis, Sandy, and the girls have you, Catrina, and me to help them get settled. From what Kianna said, her parents were from Earth, and they're confident they can lean on Kianna's grandparents for help. But, what about Jade, her sisters, and their families? What about the rest of those who've never set foot on Earth? Where'll they go?"

Braedon sighed. "Only time will tell. At least it appears that we were right about the US government being willing to offer aid. I suppose it probably helps that we brought technology with us that's a hundred years-or-so more advanced than theirs. I guess that's worth the price of relocating twenty thousand people."

"That's another thing. I'm just saddened that it was *only* twenty thousand. I mean, that's just a fifth of the population! Why would so many choose to stay, knowing that they'd be dead within a week?"

Braedon shook his head. "I overheard some of the refugees say that Mathison had already assured the populace, and even some of the governors and administrators from the other cities, that his scientists concluded that this disruption was caused by an anomaly that had been corrected. He told them the earthquakes would diminish soon, and they bought it.

"It's sad that some people are so afraid of the unknown they would rather stick with the familiar, choosing to believe those who tell them what they want to hear rather than what reality dictates," he continued. "I also heard that many felt that Pandora's Box offered them all the freedom they wanted. Knowing that there were no Box facilities here on Earth, they chose to remain. Their desire for the counterfeit overpowered their desire for the real thing. From the reports we've received, the other cities experienced the same issues."

Gunther was silent for several moments as he considered Braedon's words. "I just...I just can't get over the thought of all those people being crushed! I feel like...maybe we could've done more."

"We did everything we could. Don't take the blame for what was completely out of your control. Those people made their own decisions."

"I'm just glad we buried the Vortex in the woods before the refugees arrived," Gunther said. "I don't ever want anyone using it to create a weapon, or to try to open a portal to Tartarus, or anywhere else for that matter! When all this is settled, I'm going to return to those woods, find it, and destroy it completely!"

Braedon's eyebrows lifted. "Probably a good idea. We definitely don't want it falling into the wrong hands."

"Like jihadists?"

"Exactly," Braedon said.

"By the way," Gunther said, his face brightening, "I saw Raptor's sister, Zahra, and her husband on the news. They were among the refugees from Bab al-Jihad."

Braedon smiled. "Yeah, we received word that they made it. Here's hoping the more moderate Muslims will be able to settle in other areas that aren't radicalized. In fact, Catrina and I are petitioning to have Zahra and her family come live in the US."

"That would be great. I hope it all works out," Gunther stated.

"But hey, don't take the weight of the world on your shoulders," Braedon said, clapping Gunther on the back and helping him to stand. "Right now, it's your turn to call your wife!"

Gunther's hands shook as he nervously ran his fingers through his hair and smoothed out the wrinkles in his clothes. "Look at me! I'm shaking like a teenager who's about to ask a girl to the prom!"

The two men shared the laugh as they exited the room. A moment later, they arrived at the office within the school that had been turned into a makeshift videophone center. Inside was a desk, several chairs and a large digital tablet. Those who needed to call family or friends were assigned a timeslot. Finally, after nearly a day of waiting, Gunther's scheduled time had arrived.

As Gunther and Braedon waited in the hallway for the previous caller to finish his conversation, Gunther turned to his companion. "You and Catrina *will* come to meet Eveleen, won't you? Travis and his family will be there as well."

Braedon smiled. "Of course. But we have to see our families and find a place to get settled, first."

"Yes, yes," Gunther amended hurriedly. "I understand. I only meant that you're always welcome at my table. Perhaps we can talk sometime about your beliefs. I've never been a religious man, but...recently I've been thinking I might not know as much as I think I do."

"I'd love nothing more."

The door to the office opened and the previous occupant exited the room, his eyes filled with tears of joy. Once he had moved on down the hallway, Braedon turned to Gunther. "Did you see that? Families are being brought back together and others are experiencing a whole new world for the first time. You did that, Gunther Leuschen."

Gunther smiled, the burden on his shoulders easing a little. "We did it."

"I'll wait out here for you."

Filled with overwhelming excitement and trepidation, Gunther stepped into the office, closed the door and sat down in front of the tablet. His hands shook so much he had to input the number three times before he got it right. With each ring of the phone, his heart pounded harder and harder.

Finally, the screen flickered to life as someone on the other line picked up. Gunther felt his heart lurch into his throat as the image of the woman he had longed to see for over five years appeared on the screen.

"Hello?"

"Eveleen! It's me! Gunther!"

26

GOOD-BYES AND REUNIONS

"My friends, we've come together today to pay our respects to five men who gave their lives so that others might live—Steven Russell, Rahib Ahmed, Erik Ramsay, Xavier Traverse, and Caleb Moravec."

Braedon paused and looked out at those seated in front of him, those who had come to mean so much to him during his time in Tartarus. To his left, Gunther sat next to Travis, his wife Sandy, and their two daughters, Cage and Marissa. Behind them, Braedon saw the man that Travis had introduced to him as Juan. He soon learned that Juan was the security technician who was responsible for helping Gunther sneak into the Elysium Research and Records compound. Beside Juan was his wife and family, as well as his father. To Braedon's right sat Catrina and Jade, who in turn sat with Kianna, her daughter Alayna, and her parents.

As he scanned those who sat behind his closest friends, he saw that Steven's sister, his adult sons—Steven, Jr. and Seth—and their families had also joined the small group, as did many of Steven's Christian friends from the Elysium chapter of the Crimson Liberty organization. Although he wished Manoj and the other CL members from Dehali could be here, they were now in India and unable to make the trip. It at least brought him peace when he had received the message that they had made it to Earth safely.

"Too often, we spend the majority of our lives living in a bubble of invincibility," Braedon said, his strong voice filling the small room in which they had gathered. Due to the circumstances, the bodies of Raptor, Erik, and Xavier had already been taken to a burial site days ago. In lieu of caskets, pictures of the men were set up along one wall framed by wreaths and flowers. "We feel like death is just a story told to frighten children.

"But then one day, death comes to our doorstep and bursts our comfortable bubble, and no matter how much we wish it away, we are forced to confront the reality that someone we love is gone. It is in these moments, when the grief is strongest, that the veil is removed from our eyes and we get a glimpse at an unpleasant yet undeniable truth—we will all die someday."

Braedon paused and took a drink of water from a glass resting on the lectern before continuing. "Steven often used a phrase that quickly became a guiding principle for me as well. He said, 'The most important question we can answer in life is—what will happen when I die? How we answer this question will determine how we should live our life.' Steven found the answer to that question and changed the course of his life to match his beliefs. He challenged me to do my own research and think through my own beliefs. He challenged me not to just believe things arbitrarily, but to have *reasons* for my faith. He challenged me to study other belief systems and to ask tough questions of my own. He even challenged me to believe hard truths, even if I didn't like them.

"Friends, if you would honor Steven's memory, and the memory of our other friends and loved ones, I urge you to consider his words. Seek to answer this question while the veil is still removed. Do it before the comfortable bubble envelops you once again.

"If he were here today, I know exactly what Steven would say. In fact, you can *read* exactly what he would tell you for yourself. Before he died, he passed on to me a digital copy of a journal he wrote to his sons," Braedon said, looking toward the two men sitting near the back. He saw their expressions shift, making it clear they had never known the journal existed. "Before we go our separate ways, I'd like to give each of you a copy. Read it, and consider carefully his reasoning and wisdom.

"But for now, I'd like to summarize his conclusion. He would tell you that the answer to this most important of questions regarding what happens after death can be found in the Bible. There *is* a God who created us, yet we rebelled against him. When we are truly honest with ourselves, we recognize that rebellion in our hearts. It's that part of us that flares up from time to time and lashes out. It's that part of us we don't like—that selfish, petty, ignorant, nasty part of us. No matter how much 'good' we do to compensate for our immoral deeds, we can never get rid of the evil that resides in the core of our being. We can never bridge the gulf that exists between us and God because of our sin.

"Yet there is hope. The Bible makes it clear that because God loves us so much, he did what we couldn't do. Every other religion in the world tries to offer hope by *doing* good things. But the truth is that no amount of charity or righteousness can remove our sin. That's why God sent his Son, Jesus Christ, to pay the penalty of death, to bridge the gap between us and God. We cannot *earn* salvation, we can only accept it as a *gift*.

"Steven knew this, and this is what he wrote about in his journal. I have experienced firsthand the joy that comes when you receive the gift of salvation. It has changed my own life, and I got a front row seat to watch this truth change the life of Rahib. From the moment I met him, I saw the bitterness and anger he felt manifest itself in his actions and words. Yet, in the days that followed, I watched him change slowly. Until finally, just before his death, I saw a light begin to shine from within him. I watched as the peace he had sought for so many years came to rest in his soul.

"Friends, as I mentioned before, there are some truths that are hard to accept. I will not say for certain what has happened to Erik, Xavier, and Caleb, for only God knows what lies in the hearts of men. But the Bible does make it clear that when one who has accepted Jesus as Lord and Savior dies, he or she will go to heaven and live with him for eternity.

"I urge you today to make that decision. If you wait, the reality of your fleeting existence may fade with time, and you may once more feel invincible. None of us is promised another day of life. Again I say—if you honor the sacrifice these men made, then let their deaths serve as a catalyst that spurs you on to find the truth. Thank you."

With his remarks finished, Braedon stepped away from the lectern and returned to his seat next to Catrina. A short time later, the ceremony concluded, and everyone began to converse with one another in hushed, reverent tones.

Braedon turned to see Steven's two sons approaching, their families hanging back slightly behind them. They thanked him, and Braedon had a chance to fulfill his promise to his mentor by giving them a copy of their father's journal.

As Steven's family turned and left, Braedon spent the next half hour visiting with the members of Crimson Liberty. When the last of them had departed, he found that the room was empty except for Catrina, Kianna, Gunther, Travis, and Jade.

The six of them stood in silence for several moments before Jade finally broke the ice. "Well, I guess this is it. It's been nearly a week already, yet I still can't believe we made it to Earth."

"I know what you mean," Kianna stated. "I still have to pinch myself from time to time to make sure I'm not dreaming."

"Thank you all," Gunther said, his eyes moist with tears. "Please don't become strangers. You are always welcome at my home."

"Let's at least stay in touch through videophones," Catrina said.

Jade snickered. "It's too bad we don't have the implant feeds anymore. It feels so 'old school' to have to use a handheld device."

"It does have the added benefit of giving you a picture, though," Braedon commented.

"That's true," Jade said with a smile. "Unless it's someone you don't *want* to see! It was bad enough in Tartarus to have to hear Xavier's whining voice all the time when I used the TC channel. I think if I had to see his ugly mug as well, I would've gone insane!"

The group shared a brief moment of laughter before the ache of their absent friends dampened the mood. "I can't believe I'm going to say this, but I really miss that self-centered, pretty boy," Jade said.

"Yeah, and that big lug Charon as well," Kianna added.

They lapsed into silence once more, which was finally broken by Catrina. "We'd better get going," she said quietly to Braedon. "We need to get to the airport in a couple hours, and we still have to gather our things."

"Sure," Braedon replied. "Take care, everyone. Mingyu, have a safe trip to China. We're so glad to hear your sisters and their families made it out safe." Jade accepted his concern with a nod. "Thank you for everything. You've given me plenty to think about. I do plan to finish reading Steven's journal one of these days." "I'll be praying for you," Braedon said. Catrina and Kianna both stepped forward and embraced the Asian woman. Unaccustomed to such affection, the normally tough woman awkwardly returned their hugs.

"I'm gonna get going as well," Kianna said. "I'm flying out to meet my grandparents for the first time."

"Safe travels," Gunther said. "We must leave soon as well. Travis, Sandy, and the girls are coming with me to see Eveleen."

"Yes," Travis confirmed. "We're going to be staying with them until we can find a place of our own nearby."

Braedon looked at his friends warmly. "I know some of you may not be comfortable with this, but I'm going to ask that you indulge me anyway. I'd like to pray for us." With that, the group bowed their heads, and he prayed a blessing over them. When he finished, the friends said their final good-byes and went their separate ways.

Gunther Leuschen felt his pulse quicken and fought against the sudden rush of tears that threatened to spill down his face as he made the final turn onto the street that led to his house.

This was it! The moment he had dreamed about every night for the past five years was about to happen! He was home at last!

And waiting for him was the love of his life—his precious wife of thirty-eight years, Eveleen.

Beside him in the passenger seat, Travis couldn't help but smile. "Stop fidgeting with your tie and your hair. You're acting more nervous than a preteen girl getting ready for her first dance!"

In the backseat, Gunther heard snickering from Travis's daughters, followed by a lighthearted reprimand from their mother.

Gunther blushed. "That's almost exactly what Braedon said when I went to call her the first time. It's just...I can't wait to see her! It's like...our wedding day all over again," Gunther said, unable to prevent a solitary tear from sliding down his cheek. Wiping it quickly away, he started breathing faster as he pulled into the driveway of his house. He placed the vehicle in park, shut the engine off, and put both hands on the wheel in an effort to calm himself down. He felt the slight pressure of a gentle hand on his shoulder and turned to see Sandy smiling at him.

"Go get her, tiger!"

He returned her smile, then fumbled with the handle of the door, his shaking hands making even that simple task difficult. A moment later, he stood outside the vehicle, his eyes glued on the front of the simple ranch house. Although he vaguely heard the other car doors open and close, signaling that Travis and his family had also exited the vehicle, his attention was focused solely on the door of the house as it began to open.

There—standing in the doorway not more than twenty feet away, dressed in a beautifully embroidered white dress with light pink flower patterns—stood Eveleen. For a moment, neither could move as tears ran freely down both their cheeks. Finally, like two magnets being pulled toward one another, husband and wife ran forward and fell into each other's arms.

Caught up in the reunion, Travis held Sandy close and fought against his own tears of joy. His daughters cried openly at the touching display of affection from the older couple. Other family members and friends who had come to welcome Gunther home spilled out of the house and onto the lawn. Several of the women cupped their hands over their mouths as they were caught up in the moment.

Overwhelmed by emotion, Gunther's knees trembled. He sank down onto the grass, pulling his wife with him. For an entire minute, the two simply held one another, wept, kissed, and caressed each other's faces. At last, as if suddenly realizing they had an audience, they laughed sheepishly and rose to their feet to warm applause.

Immediately, Gunther and Eveleen were surrounded by their friends and loved ones. The nightmare that had begun in the quiet forest five years ago was now just a memory. Gunther was home.

EPILOGUE

Kianna stepped out of the car and stood for several moments staring at the quiet, split-level house in the north suburbs of Chicago. She suddenly felt the small hand of her eight-year-old daughter slip into hers. She had been so focused on her own thoughts that she hadn't even noticed that Alayna had exited the car. Turning, she smiled down at her.

"Grandma and Grandpa said it might help if I went with you," Alayna said.

"Yes, I think it might," Kianna replied. Holding onto her daughter's hand to keep her own from shaking, the two of them made their way up the walkway toward the house. Taking a deep breath, Kianna rang the doorbell.

They were greeted instantly by the sound of two dogs barking hysterically. To their left, the tan-colored curtains that covered the large bay window rippled, then revealed the pointy snouts of two golden retrievers that looked to be less than a year old. A man's voice could be heard shouting at the dogs from inside the house. "Cut it out, both of you. Alan, Aaron, get those mutts in the kitchen for me, will ya?"

Beside her, Kianna heard Alayna giggle as the dogs' noses disappeared suddenly and the barking became noticeably quieter. A moment later, the door of the house opened to reveal an African American man in his early fifties with graying hair and neatly trimmed moustache. The moment his eyes fell upon the two visitors, they widened with shock, and his face paled noticeably.

As he stood there in stunned silence, a woman's voice came from behind him. "Is it her?" A second later, the door opened wider as the woman appeared next to her husband, her own face instantly mirroring his surprise and amazement.

It took a moment for the woman to find her voice again. When she finally spoke, her words were barely a whisper, as if anything more would cause the visitors to suddenly vanish into thin air. "Joy? Joy…is it really you? And this…" she said, turning to look at Alayna, "is this…our granddaughter?"

Kianna's expression filled with compassion as she smiled warmly. "No, I'm sorry. My name is Kianna, and this is my daughter Alayna."

The couple's expressions immediately fell. "Pardon us," the woman said. "It's just…we're expecting visitors today, and you… you both bear a striking resemblance to our daughter. You see, she was one of those who were taken through the portals eight years ago to that…that other world. I'm sure you heard about it on the news."

"Yes, we have," Kianna said. "In fact, we *are* here because of that."

At her pronouncement, the couple both frowned and exchanged glances. "Really?" the man asked in confusion. "How so? What can we do for you?"

Kianna paused, her heart racing. *Please, Lord, help them understand,* she prayed. "We're both here on behalf of your daughter. Joy and her husband are waiting in the car."

At this, the woman placed her hand over her mouth and swayed to the side, causing her husband to put an arm around her to steady her. Immediately, the couple glanced toward the car. However, from their angle, they could only make out the shapes of two people sitting in the backseat.

"Where's my little girl?" the woman asked, her voice cracking. "Why...why haven't they come out to greet us?"

Unable to contain herself, Kianna felt tears springing into her eyes and she fought to control her voice. "Because...because she wanted me to explain something to you both first."

"What's wrong? What happened to her down there?" the man said frantically. "Is she okay?"

"She's completely healthy and still stunningly beautiful," Kianna said, her heart breaking.

"I don't get it then. What's going on?"

"In the news reports about the refugees from Tartarus, did you hear about the time difference between there and Earth?" Kianna asked.

"Yes, of course," the man said, his brow furrowing in confusion. "They said something about...one year on Earth was the same as five years there. So? What does this have to do with..." He suddenly stopped as the truth dawned on him. He looked down at Kianna and Alayna as if seeing them with new eyes. "Oh...my..."

"What is it?" the woman said, her husband's reaction filling her with dread.

At that moment, the back door of the car opened. Slowly, a man and woman filed out and closed the door behind them, their eyes fixed on where Kianna stood.

"Mommy? Daddy?" the woman said, her lower jaw quivering. Letting go of her husband's hand, Joy ran as fast as she could up the walkway and fell into the arms of her parents. It was only then that her mother realized the horrible truth.

Although Joy had been only nineteen years old when she had been taken to Tartarus eight years ago, due to the time change between worlds, she had spent a full forty years in the underground world and was now *older* than her parents!

Kianna picked up Alayna and held her close, the two of them watching the bittersweet reunion in silence. They waited patiently for several minutes, their own tears spilling down their cheeks. Finally, the man looked once more toward the two guests. "So then, you two must be our...our granddaughter and...great-granddaughter!"

Unable to speak, Kianna merely smiled and nodded. The man immediately enveloped the two of them in a warm embrace, then drew back to look at them in amazement. "Please forgive our manners. This is a wonderful occasion." He gestured toward Joy's husband, Franklin. "Come in, all of you. We're so thrilled to meet you. I'm Jerome, and this is my wife Tarswha, but you can call us Grandpa and Grandma. Welcome to the Freeman clan! Come on inside and meet the rest of the family. I also want to introduce you to my best friend, Jeffrey, and his wife, Rebecca."

With that, he led them into the house. Kianna offered up a quick prayer of thanks to God, then stepped into the house with her daughter in order to meet the rest of her new family.

Afterword

Eternity. We can't even fathom the truths contained in that one word. In this material world, everything we see has a beginning and an end. Even our universe itself had a beginning. Yet many make the mistake of thinking that death is the end. But if we base our worldview on the Bible, we will quickly realize that death is *not* the end. We are *not* mortal beings. We are *immortal*. We will live forever. The only question is: where will we spend that eternity?

Our modern culture loves to talk about heaven—paradise—a place with no more suffering or pain, a place where we can be reunited with loved ones. At funerals, well-meaning people often make statements like, "She's in a better place." Movies and TV shows make it clear that, as long as you were a 'good' person, then you'll be accepted into heaven.

But we don't like to talk about hell or sin. In fact, the same pop culture sends us the message that if hell is real at all, it is a place for only the worst of people, like Hitler, Stalin, serial killers and the like. And more than likely, the concept of hell itself was just something priests used in the middle ages to exploit the masses and keep them dependent on the church for salvation and forgiveness.

What is the truth? What does the Bible say about hell?

It is beyond the scope of these author's notes to give a full treatise on the subject. However, there are several things that the Bible makes very clear. One of them is found in John 14:6. Jesus says, "I am the way and the truth and the life. No one comes to the father except through me."

Many scoff at this idea, thinking that Christians are arrogant to believe that their religion is correct and that all others are wrong. But what they fail to realize is that *all* religions are exclusive to a point. When you make a truth claim, which all religions do, then you are being exclusive. In a courtroom drama, if someone says, "The butler did it!" then they are making a truth claim, excluding all other suspects.

HINDU PARABLE

Yet many don't see the logical fallacy in claiming that "all religions lead to God." They use the famous Hindu parable about the blind men and the elephant, which goes something like this:

> A group of blind men were led to an elephant to touch it and describe what it is like. One blind man touched the trunk and said, "It is like a tree branch!" Another touched the leg and exclaimed, "It is like a pillar." Yet another touched the ear and said, "It is like a canvas." Finally, another touched the tail and said, "It is like a rope."

The moral of the parable is that, like the blind men, each religion sees "God" in a different way. They only understand a part of God, but no one has the whole truth. At first, this parable seems wise. However, if you think about it for a little longer, you will realize it really doesn't explain what it initially seems to explain. Although each blind man understood what a portion of the elephant was like, the truth is that *all the blind men were wrong!*

What the parable is *really* teaching is that, if one claims that all religions lead to God, what they really mean is that all religions are *wrong* about God. This actually makes sense considering the logical law of non-contradiction. Since the religions of the world make contradictory truth claims, then in order to keep with the law of non-contradiction, you have only two options: either one religion is the truth and the rest are false, or they are *all* wrong.

That isn't to say that *everything* a religion teaches is false, just like the blind men were correct in a small way. But the main doctrines of those religions are false in the same way that an elephant as a whole is not like a pillar, a rope, etc. When you compare the truth claims of the major religions of the world, you quickly see that they are *substantially* different and, at best, *superficially* the same.

Of all the religions of the world, only Christianity makes a truth claim that can be verified through logic and archeology (see the author's notes in the first three books in *The Tartarus Chronicles*).

Therefore, it is not illogical to make the statement that those who do not accept the free gift of salvation that is offered to all through Jesus's sacrifice on the cross will not be saved any more than to state "the butler did it!"

With that said, I would like to offer a word of caution. We humans do not know what is in another person's heart nor do we know every thought a person has ever had. Therefore, we can never be certain whether or not a person has repented before death. We should be careful to never make a claim that a person went to hell. We can have personal assurance of heaven, but it is not our place to try to say what is in another's heart.

While there are differing views regarding hell and many questions we struggle to find answers to, there are also many truths of which we can be certain based on scripture: Jesus's death provided the only means for salvation. God is just and will judge each accordingly. Those who do not accept him will not be saved. We should do our best to share these truths with others in the hopes that they will find salvation.

TRUTHS FROM THE LABYRINTH

Like the Labyrinth in this story, our lives are filled with seemingly endless choices. Each day, we have to decide which path to take. Some paths lead to dangers, others to beauty and safety. We must navigate through our lives carefully and weigh each decision. But God has not left us without directions. The Bible is like the map to the Labyrinth. If we allow his Word to guide our decisions, we can walk with confidence. Psalm 119:105 says, "Your word is a lamp for my feet, a light on my path." Like Braedon and Raptor facing the Viper Lizards and lava flow deep in the bowels of the Labyrinth, sometimes God leads us through difficult trials in order to ultimately bring us to safety or salvation. As long as we keep our eyes on him, we can trust he will lead us through.

Yet if we choose to ignore his guidance, we will find ourselves lost in this world, being devoured by our own wrong choices and caught in the traps of the enemy. We must know his Word and study it diligently. It is our guide.

As much as we often don't like to think about the doctrine of hell, we must keep it fresh in our minds for the sake of those we love that are unsaved. Think for a moment. Did it bother you as a reader that some of the characters that you have (hopefully) come to care for were devoured by the dragon? If so, how much more should it bother us that real people are dying every day and facing judgment? As much as I wanted to tell a story with an idyllic happy ending, that would have further propagated the lie that as long as someone is a 'good' person, he or she will go to heaven.

Finally, I want to make it clear that, while the dragon does represent Satan in this story, according to the Bible, the dragon himself will face judgment.

Although First Peter 5:8 states that, "Your enemy the devil prowls around like a roaring lion looking for someone to devour," in truth, Revelation 20 shows that ultimately, he will be "devoured" himself. Hell is not a place where the devil and demons take joy in torturing humans. The enemy of our souls will one day receive punishment that he deserves.

FINAL THOUGHTS

Reader, it is my prayer that the information I have presented in *The Tartarus Chronicles* will prick your interest and lead you to discover more. I also pray that, if you have not already accepted what Jesus did to purchase your salvation, you would be moved to do so.

And if you are already a Christian, I pray that these books will have strengthened your faith and given you answers so that you will "always be prepared to give an answer to everyone who asks you to give the reason for the hope that you have."

In his service,

Keith A. Robinson
October 2, 2016

SUGGESTED RESOURCES

BOOKS

The Case for Christ by Lee Strobel
The Case for Faith by Lee Strobel
The Case for a Creator by Lee Strobel
Evidence That Demands a Verdict by Josh McDowell
World Religions in a Nutshell by Ray Comfort
World Religions and Cults: Counterfeits of Christianity (Volume 1), by Bodie Hodge and Roger Patterson

WEBSITES

Apologetics Fiction (www.apologeticsfiction.com), the official website for Keith A. Robinson.
Apologetics 315 (www.apologetics315.com), a great hub listing other apologetics websites, podcasts, and articles.
Probe (www.probe.org), the website for Probe Ministries, full of great articles and materials.
Lee Strobel (www.leestrobel.com), the official website for Lee Strobel; also full of great videos, articles, etc.
Answers in Genesis (www.answersingenesis.org): Although this

website has mostly articles that deal with creation and evolution, there are many other great videos and articles available on a variety of topics regarding Christianity.

Living Waters (www.livingwaters.com), the website for Ray Comfort and Kirk Cameron's ministry.

Other Books by Keith A. Robinson

THE ORIGINS TRILOGY

Book 1: *Logic's End* – In 2034, Rebecca Evans travels to a distant planet searching for life. But when she arrives, she finds a world where survival of the fittest is played out to its logical end. Forced to accept help from mutated animal-like creatures, Rebecca struggles to get off the planet, and soon begins to question everything she once believed about evolution.

Book 2: *Pyramid of the Ancients* – Four years after *Logic's End*, Rebecca's husband, Jeffrey, discovers a mysterious two-story pyramid buried in the sands of Iraq, which turns out to be a machine. When activated, it takes Rebecca, Jeffrey, and a team of scientists backward into time on a journey that challenges their theories about the history of the earth.

Book 3: Escaping the Cataclysm – Picking up where *Pyramid* leaves off, the team fights against all odds to escape from the time just before Noah's flood and return to the future.

ABOUT KEITH A. ROBINSON

AUTHOR OF *THE ORIGINS TRILOGY* AND *THE TARTARUS CHRONICLES*

Keith Robinson has dedicated his life to teaching others how to defend the Christian faith. Since the release of *Logic's End*, his first novel, he has been a featured speaker at Christian music festivals, homeschool conventions, apologetics seminars, and churches, as well as appearing as a guest on numerous radio shows.

Since completing his Origins Trilogy, Mr. Robinson has been working on *The Tartarus Chronicles*, a new series of action/adventure novels dealing with the topic of world religions and worldviews.

When not writing or speaking, Mr. Robinson is the full-time public school orchestra director at the Kenosha School of Technology Enhanced Curriculum, and he is a professional freelance violist and violinist in the Southeastern Wisconsin/Northeastern Illinois area. He currently resides in Kenosha, Wisconsin, with his wife, Stephanie, their five children, and a Rottweiler named Thor.

For more information, visit www.ApologeticsFiction.com.

Made in the USA
Middletown, DE
14 June 2022

67062641R00129